THE NURSERY MAID

The tea shop was open, and Charles led the
way to a small marble-topped table. He ordered
tea and cakes for himself and Polly.

He was fully aware that what he was doing
was reprehensible, and if it should ever reach
Lady Augusta's ears he would be asked to
leave at once. But he was in a reckless mood,
and he did not care a straw for Lady
Augusta. In fact, he hoped she would hear
that he had given one of her housemaids a
cup of tea in Market Broughton in broad
daylight.

About Polly herself, and how such an
escapade might affect her, he did not think
at all . . .

The Nursery Maid

Mary Ann Gibbs

CORONET BOOKS
Hodder and Stoughton

First published in Great Britain in 1963 by
Hurst and Blackett Limited

Coronet edition 1975

Printed and bound in Great Britain for
Coronet Books, Hodder and Stoughton,
St. Paul's House, Warwick Lane,
London, EC4P 4AH
By C. Nicholls & Company Ltd,
The Philips Park Press, Manchester

ISBN 0 340 19944 X

IT was the first of January in the year 1889 when Polly Kettle started in service at Windover Manor. All the night before she lay awake, listening to the familiar sounds in the cottage where she had lived most of her life, as the old year died and her aunt moved about downstairs finishing her ironing by candlelight. Her brother-in-law, Polly's Uncle Ebenezer, would drop the basket of washing off at the Rectory when he took Polly to Windover in the morning. It was a very large basket of washing and all very beautifully done, because Polly's Aunt Ada earned two shillings a week for doing it, and the Rector's wife in Moccrington village wouldn't pay all that for her laundry unless it was done to her satisfaction. She was a very particular lady, was the Rector's wife, and very free with her advice. It was she who had told Polly's Aunt Ada that she ought to get that niece of hers into a place as soon as possible, and that she would take her at the Rectory as between-maid when the time came. But Aunt Ada had heard that the food was scarce down at the Rectory and she had said she could not spare Polly yet.

Even Aunt Ada's footsteps stopped at last on that closing night of 1888, and she came upstairs and the rumbling snore of Uncle Reuben broke off for a moment and then began again louder than ever as his wife got ready to get into bed. She moved quietly so that she should not disturb the children who slept in the tiny back bedroom next door, the three little girls sharing the big bed with Polly, and the two little boys on a mattress on the floor.

Polly lay still, because the wall between the rooms was paper-thin, and she knew her aunt would worry if she thought she was lying awake. Ever since Uncle Reuben had been ill one Christmas and nearly died, Aunt Ada had worried over everything: where the rent was coming from, how she was to find food for them all, and what she was to do when their clothes and their boots wore out, and, more than anything else, what would happen to the children if she should fall ill and die too.

Uncle Reuben got better, however, and was soon able to continue his work as drover with Farmer Johnson on the other side of Moccrington, but it didn't stop Aunt Ada from worrying, because worry becomes a habit once it is started, and if she could have taken in twice the amount of washing she would have done so and put a little money by week by week.

Polly attempted to combat her fears as she grew older and because she was the eldest of the children her aunt listened to her and relied on her to help her with them all.

"I don't know what I shall do when you're gone, Polly," she said only that day as she held the iron near her face to test its heat. "I don't indeed."

"But I shan't be far away," Polly said. Windover was only fifteen miles away as the crow flies, and eighteen by road. "And there'll be one less mouth to feed, Auntie, and you and Uncle Reuben won't have to find me any more clothes. Once I've paid you back from my wages for all you've spent on setting me up I'll be able to keep myself and send you a little money too every month. I won't forget you, Auntie, nor Uncle Reuben, nor how good you've both been to me. And little Janie will help you with the smaller ones. She's getting very handy is Janie, and she's good with the others, though she does boss them so much."

"I shall miss you all the same, my dear," said her aunt with a sigh, thinking of the Rectory place that had been going begging with regret now that it was too late, and banging down her iron on the Rector's shirts.

It was a couple of months now since Polly had been to see her other aunt, Mrs. Phillips, in Market Broughton, five miles away, and happened to find Mrs. Grim with her that day.

Mrs. Phillips was a very important person in the family

because she owned her own greengrocery business, and lived with Uncle Ebenezer over the shop with a girl to help her. Uncle Ebenezer, being a carrier, was out all day, and all the week his wife served in the shop with a sacking apron tied round her waist and one of her husband's caps turned back to front on her head above the curlers in her fringe.

But on Sundays she shed the curlers and the cap and the apron and came out in all her Sabbath glory of black satin, with her fringe a frizz on her high forehead wonderful to behold, and a large Cairngorm brooch pinned in to the bosom of the dress, supporting a gold watch-chain. The watch-chain belonged to a gold watch, which was tucked into the waist of her dress, and both had been a reward for many years' service in a noble household, where she had been head housemaid before she left to marry Uncle Ebenezer.

On Sundays Aunt Hannah Phillips went to chapel in the morning and again in the evening, while the girl cooked the midday dinner and waited on her master and mistress at table just as if they were gentry. Once in every six months or so Polly was invited over on a Sunday to share this dinner, and because the five miles into the town from Moccrington was a long and lonely walk over the bleak, flat fen country, she came to the meal with such an appetite that her aunt would exclaim:

"Bless you, child, I would rather keep you a week than a fortnit! How poor Ada manages, I do not know!"

It did not occur to her to relieve her sister of their orphaned niece, although she had no children herself and Ada had five of her own besides Polly, but at the end of the day, when Uncle Ebenezer drove her home in his cart while Aunt Hannah was in chapel, the back of it held a goodly load of vegetables and fruit left over from the week before. And if the oranges were a bit dry or mildewed, and the bananas brown and soft, the children did not mind, but received them with delight for the luxuries that they were. And with it all there would often be a rabbit, or a couple of pigeons, or a boiling fowl, that Uncle Ebenezer had picked up on his rounds, because he was a kindly man and had much Christian charity in his soul, even if he wasn't much of a one for chapel-going.

On his way home he would stop at the Cat and Fiddle in Moccrington and tether his horse to the drinking trough outside while he lowered a quart or so of beer. The Cat and Fiddle had very good beer, and as he smacked his lips over it the landlord's wife would enquire respectfully after Hannah.

Uncle Ebenezer also had great respect for his wife: her claim to gentility was supported by him with due humility, and he shared her reverence for the great family in which she had been privileged to serve. Had not his lordship given her the gold watch and chain, and fifty pounds besides, when she married, so that she had been able to start her greengrocery business, and had never looked back from that moment?

Hannah still kept up with some of her old friends, however, and among them was Mrs. Grim, who had been still-room maid in the same house when they were young, and was now housekeeper to Lady Augusta Harroby at Windover Manor. It was to this important lady that Polly's Aunt Hannah spoke about her niece that Sunday afternoon in November, while Polly was helping the girl to wash the dishes in the kitchen.

"The child's not quite fourteen," she said. "But she's a quick, neat little creature. I'd like her to go into good service, Lizzie. She'd go far, would Polly, and, what is more, in a house like yours she would get enough to eat. The Rector's lady at Moccrington was anxious to have her last summer, but Ada wouldn't let her go, and I must say I thought she was wise. The Rectory at Moccrington's got the name for skimping on food—stewed bones in the kitchen and no butter and the milk watered down—and that's no good for a poor little scrap like Polly. Did you see her at her dinner? She ate as if she was starving, and in spite of her love for the child, with all those children of her own to feed I'm sure Ada wouldn't be sorry to see her go now, if she could be sure she was going to a good place."

"She don't look over strong," said Mrs. Grim doubtfully. "And it's another kitchen-maid that we're wanting at the moment. I had in mind a bigger and stronger girl than Polly, because there's a mint of scrubbing and scouring of all our big stone floors, and that's without counting the great cauldrons of vegetables she'd have to do as well. . . . But I'm willing to give her a trial, as long as her aunt don't want more'n five shillings a month for her. I couldn't see my way to paying more than that."

"And I know Ada wouldn't expect it," said Mrs. Phillips in a tone of satisfaction, and then she frowned. "But wait, there's the clothes to be found. . . . Would Ada have to supply very many for her, Lizzie? I don't think she would have the money to lay out on much in that line."

"I supply her with her print dresses and black, and caps and aprons," said Mrs. Grim crisply. "But I expect my girls to find their own stockings—three pair best black wool, Hannah—and all underclothes and night-gowns, and a good stout pair of boots. I know it comes a burden on the girls' mothers at first to put down the money for that outlay, but it keeps young maids steady and stops them from getting too homesick. They don't run home because they know that if they do they won't get a character from me, and their mothers will be left with a debt of thirty shillings to pay off, and nothing coming in every month to settle it."

Mrs. Phillips considered Polly's outgrown clothes and felt even more doubtful: Ada could not possibly find so much. Why, black stockings would cost at least one and elevenpence a pair, and the boots the best part of five shillings—it was no use paying less because the soles were just brown paper—and the cheapest calico for underclothes and night-gowns would be all of threepence a yard, if not sixpence. Ada would have to pay down the best part of thirty shillings, as Mrs. Grim had said, and Reuben's wages weren't more than seven-and-sixpence.

"Well," she said unwillingly, her natural kindness as usual at war with her dislike for spending money, "if that's how it is to be, Lizzie, I might buy Polly's clothes myself and let Ada keep her wages when the time comes, to pay her back a little for all these years of her keep. The poor woman won't say no to it, I'm certain."

"Don't tell Polly what you are doing, then," warned Mrs. Grim, as she folded back her skirt and stretched her toes to the sitting-room fire. "Otherwise she might think she owed nothing to nobody, and it isn't good to bring a girl up to be thriftless. Teach 'em to save when they're young, my dear, and give them a sense of responsibility to them that has brought them up and you won't live to regret it." She paused, her eyes going sharply to her friend. "What was Polly's mother like?" she asked curiously.

Mrs. Phillips frowned.

"A poor feckless creature," she said abruptly. She had also died in the Union, but wild horses would not drag that admission of disgrace from her. "But that's what comes of marrying a soldier. 'He won't be no good to you, Tilda,' I said, when I heard she was walking out with him. 'Soldiers' wives never have a penny piece, and when the babies come along what will you do then? You can't look after yourself, let alone a family in the married quarters of a barracks!' She never had a notion of how to turn work over, hadn't Tilda, and they're that strict in army barracks, Lizzie. If a soldier's wife is untidy her life isn't worth living. But she wouldn't listen to me, of course. She was a pretty girl, and flighty—though she didn't mean to be. Never rose to be more than a general servant, didn't Tilda, with at the most a boy to run errands. She never knew what good service was."

"What happened to her husband?" asked Mrs. Grim, and Hannah drew herself up, guessing what was in her mind.

"He was killed while practicing on the firing range on the Woolwich marshes," she said. "Something exploded in the poor man's face and blew him to pieces. . . . The regiment collected for Tilda—she had her marriage lines, make no mistake about that!—but, as I said, she was feckless, and, with the baby coming and all, it seemed as if she just couldn't take much notice of what was going on round her. I tried to rouse her and so did Ada, but it wasn't no good. When Polly was born she just took and turned her face to the wall and died."

"And your sister Ada adopted Polly?"

"Ada took her in, because, as she said, she and Reuben had been married for ten years without sight or sign of a child of their own, and the cottage was big enough for her and them. And then, as is often the way with them as tempts Providence in that way, no sooner had little Polly been with them more'n a year than Ada's own children began to arrive, ever so quick, and one after the other, all five of them. It's a queer thing that, Lizzie, and I've often thought about it, sitting here like this on a winter afternoon and looking into the fire, as we're doing now. There's some women can't seem to have children and pine after them for years, and then when they makes up their minds to adopt a child, as Ada did with Polly, blest if they don't have all they want and more. It's as if the Almighty says to them: 'So you aren't satisfied with what I've got in mind for you, my dear? Well, have your own way, then, and see what you can make of it, and don't come whining to Me now there's all them extra mouths to feed.' "

"I only had one child, as you know, Hannah," said Mrs. Grim. "And that was born dead, and after that I said never no more. Fortunately Grim was of the same opinion. He died," she added, "of drink, though I wouldn't say so to everyone." She paused, her eyes on the fire. "Our present scullery-maid is staying until after the Christmas house-party, so that Polly can come to us on New Year's Day. If Mr. Phillips will leave her with her box at Windover station I will send one of our men with the trap or the wagonette to meet her and bring her on to the Manor."

So between them did the two women settle Polly Kettle's future, and now the last day of the old year had ended, and the first of the new had begun.

When the year was only an hour old Polly heard the wild geese flying over on their way out to sea, and the sound of their wings was comforting and homely, because it was one of the sounds she had grown up with from babyhood.

Always when she heard that noise she would see them, far above the cottage roof, keeping in the V that they made behind their leader, and tonight she thought of them against the starry sky, the frosty air making the stars brighter than the sparkle of summer sunshine on the river, winking and twinkling up there around the flying geese.

And thinking about them and the black fen country over which they travelled, her excitement and apprehension suddenly left her and she fell asleep.

2

EBENEZER was to call for Polly at ten o'clock. Mrs. Grim had written to Mrs. Phillips to tell her that if the carrier could leave his niece at Windover railway station during the afternoon a conveyance from the Manor would be meeting the four-thirty train from London there, and Polly could continue her journey beside the coachman.

Windover seemed a long way away that morning over the hard, frozen roads, and the snow that had been threatening over Christmas had already begun to fall in thin, icy flakes on New Year's Eve, making the surface treacherous for horses. Ebenezer had parcels to deliver in out-of-the-way places, and he reckoned that if he were to fetch up at Windover station at four-thirty he had best collect Polly early and take her with him for most of the day.

Polly did not keep him waiting: she was watching for him from the cottage window, her black straw hat sitting crookedly on her fair head, with the yellow hair already slipping from the bun that her aunt had shown her only that morning how to fasten with hairpins at the back of her neck. The black jacket she was wearing looked far too thin for the winter weather, but her gray skirt was long and reached to her ankles, and under it her legs were encased in the new black woollen stockings and the stout new boots. The skirt had originally belonged to her Aunt Hannah, and although Ada had done her best with it, it still hung on her slight figure like a sack.

But her basket hold-all was packed and ready, and even her cotton gloves were on her hands as she gave her aunt and cousins a final hug and ran out to the cart, climbing up dexterously beside Uncle Ebenezer and tucking herself under the dry sacks that he put over her knees.

The canvas hood kept the worst of the wind off as they started out, but it still managed to make her eyes water as she leaned out to wave to the group of children who watched her go.

She was glad to scramble down to knock at doors and help with the loading and unloading of parcels: it restored the circulation to hands and feet that were rapidly becoming frozen as they travelled on. The country had never looked so unfriendly, or colder than it did today: the furrows in the black fields were full of ice, with patches of thin snow, the skeletons of the trees outlined against a yellow sky heavy with more falls to come, while the gulls flew inland, screaming, and settling on the frozen fields trying to find food.

Everything wore an air of waiting and expectancy, anticipating the moment when winter would get a closer grip, and only the sails of the windmills moved, helped by the bitter wind.

Until midday Polly was kept too busy to think much about what lay ahead of her, but after they had stopped for a bite to eat at a small public house that went by the name of The Swinging Gate, and she saw a signpost opposite that said it was only four and a half miles to Windover railway station, and she knew that they were nearly there, her stomach turned over, and the palms of her hands pricked, and she wished that she knew something more about the great house that awaited her and all the other servants in it.

Stories related by her Aunt Hannah floated back to her mind, jumbled up and terrifying. Stories of grasping housekeepers, and drunken butlers, and bullying upper servants, and bad-tempered cooks. She knew enough of Mrs. Grim to be able to trust her and to know that she would treat her fairly and well, but all she knew of the butler was that his name was Mr. Harris and that he was very strict, and that when the Squire and Lady Augusta had lords and such to visit at the Manor neither Mr. Harris nor Mrs. Grim would allow any of the maids to sit down to their dinner in the servants' hall in their caps and aprons. They had to change their dresses for dinner just as the gentry did, while the under-servants waited on them. And she knew even less about Cook, for whom she was to work in the kitchen. She hoped that she was not bad-tempered, but here, alas, her hopes were doomed to disappointment, because Cook was very bad-tempered indeed.

The wagonette had been sent to Windover station to meet young Mr. Charles Harroby, and when the head groom, Peters, who was driving it, caught sight of Uncle Ebenezer's cart, he left the horses in charge of the young man who had come with him to help with the luggage, and came over to talk to him.

"The train isn't in yet," he said. "Reckon her'll be late. Her usually is. We've brought the wagonette because her ladyship has taken the carriage horses to go paying calls, and Sir John, 'e's off shooting wild duck today down on the marshes, so there's another pair of horses gone there, to draw the brake. There was only these two left, and the wagonette to meet Mr. Charles. But I dessay he'll want to ride on the box-seat along of me and take the reins, and the girl can travel inside along of the luggage and young James. He don't ever open his mouth don't James, so he won't offend."

Polly got down from the cart and smiled at him timidly, and his eyes studied her critically.

"You don't look very old," he remarked. "What is your age, my dear?"

"Please, sir, I'm nearly fourteen," said Polly.

"You don't look it, then. And you needn't call me 'sir'. Keep that for Mr. 'Arris, the butler. He'll expect it, and I don't. I'm Peters, I am, head groom up at the Manor. Young Mr. Charles allus looks for me to meet his train when he comes to stay at Windover, because I taught him to ride and to 'old the reins. Very fond of me, is young Mr. Charles!"

Polly said nothing, but her eyes went from the old groom to the lad at the horses' heads: it was nearly dark now, and by the light from the carriage lamps she could see that he was tall and broad-shouldered under the dark green livery that he wore, and that his cockaded hat was set firmly on a dark, curly head. A bell rang inside the stationmaster's office, and Peters said he reckoned that was "her" signal, and Uncle Ebenezer said goodbye to his niece.

"I know you'll be a good girl and work hard," he said gruffly. "But there'll be times maybe when it's not all jam, even up there at that great house, with as much as you want to eat an' all. So it may help when you're feeling homesick to know as your old Uncle Ebenezer's a-thinking of you, Polly, my love, as he jogs round the countryside in this little ole cart." He kissed her, his scrubby beard tickling her cheek, and then he climbed up on his cart and moved off into the early darkness of the winter afternoon.

The train was now approaching, and Peters left the new kitchen-maid to stand by the wagonette while he went on to the platform to greet the Manor's guest. The train overshot the little platform and had to come back, with much puffing from its smoke-stack and much clanking of chains and buffers as it shunted along the single pair of rails. Then it stopped again with a creaking groan and a hiss of steam from the engine, and doors were flung open down its length, and Polly heard a cheerful voice saying:

"Hullo, Peters! I hoped you'd be here to meet me. You don't look a day older, either. Have you brought a mild old creature for me to drive?"

"I've got Darby and Joan out in the shafts, Mr. Charles," said Peters. "I had to bring the wagonette, but you needn't be frit of they. Darby and Joan won't shy at nothing, they won't."

"I wonder they can stand up by this time!" said the cheerful voice. "How long is it since I was here last, three or four years? And they were old then."

"There's a good bit of life in them still, Mr. Charles, and Squire won't hear of 'em being put down."

"I should think not indeed! Might as well have *you* put down, Peters! And who's that at their heads? Not young James Burke, promoted from stable-lad to groom! I say, how you've shot up, James. I wouldn't have recognized you!" And Mr. Charles was there beside them, a slenderly built, tall young man with fair hair and the flowing moustache of the day, and clad in a tweed suit and over-coat that exuded a pleasant smell of heather and tobacco. The overcoat had a fur collar to it, his gloves were of the finest leather, his malacca cane had a gold top to it, and his boots were as shining as if they were newly brushed: there was in fact only one thing lacking about Mr. Charles: he brought no manservant with him, because his widowed mother could not afford menservants in her household. At the Manor, therefore, the butler instructed the head footman, Everitt, to wait on the young gentle-man, which annoyed Charles not a little, as he was quite accustomed to packing and unpacking his own clothes, and the superiority of Everitt overawed him. But in what-ever light he might have appeared to the Squire's head footman, to little Polly Kettle, standing there in the darkness outside the circle of light shed by the carriage lamps, Charles was a god from another planet.

After a respectful touching of his hat to the Squire's young cousin, the silent James Burke waited until he had climbed up to the coachman's seat and turned up his coat collar against the wind before gathering the reins into his hands, and then he left the horses' heads and hurried off to help the porter with the luggage. Nobody seemed to see Polly or to know that she was there: she might have been a crate of chickens or a bale of hay that had to be fetched from the parcels office.

The luggage that was brought out and stowed away in the wagonette amazed her by its quantity and variety. Portmanteaux and Gladstone bags, shirt-boxes and hat-boxes, and rugs strapped round bundles of umbrellas and walking sticks, gun-cases and a pair of skates, a hamper with Fortnum and Mason on its label, and a Yorkshire ham sewn up in a canvas bag, all seemed to point to the fact that young Mr. Harroby was expecting to enjoy a lengthy stay at Windover. And when it had all been stored away and it came to Polly's turn, there was only room for her to sit squeezed in between it all, nursing her hold-all on her lap, while James perched himself on the largest portmanteau as easily as if he were accustomed to this form of riding, as no doubt he was.

Mr. Charles Harroby, looking back over his shoulder into the wagonette to see that all his belongings were made safe before he started off, glanced at Polly and her hold-all with some astonishment.

"And who is this?" he asked. Before she had time to gasp out a confused reply Peters answered for her.

"She's the new scullery-maid at the Manor, sir," he said. "We would have sent the servants' omnibus for her, but there was nobody to drive it except young James there, and I wouldn't trust him with a load like that on these slippery roads, good as he is with the reins. But she'll ride along of he and the luggage quite snug if you've no objection, sir."

"None in the least," said Charles kindly, and he turned back again to the more important business of taking the wagonette out of the yard.

The horses' hoofs slithered and slipped over the frozen ground, the lighted station doorway receded, and the wagonette and its load was swallowed whole by the blackness of country roads, the lamps on the carriage outlining the verge where the snowy grass met the road and that was all. Hedges could soon only be guessed at beyond the grass, and the trees noted by the sighing wind in the branches.

Although the luggage, topped by James's broad shoulders, kept the wind off her a little, Polly's hands in their cotton gloves were soon so frozen that she lost all sense of feeling, and she began to wonder if, when the hold-all finally left them, her fingers would go with it, because they did not feel as if they belonged to her any more.

The wagonette had no cover to it, and she missed the shelter of Uncle Ebenezer's cart and the warm sacks over her knees. It was not long before she was shaking with cold, and the hold-all began to rattle against the trunks on which James was sitting. He turned his head then in her direction, his eyes peering down at her.

"You're fair starved with cold!" he said, the words coming slow and gentle for so large a lad.

"Only a little bit," stammered Polly through her chattering teeth. "I'll be all right when we get there."

He put his hand on her shoulder and felt it shaking under the thin jacket and he said: "If you'll stand up a minute there's a rug under that cushion you're sitting on. I'll get it out and put it round you."

"Stand up!" chattered Polly in alarm. "B . . . but the horses are going too fast . . . I'd fall out!"

"Not if you hold on to me." He took the hold-all from her and put it on top of the portmanteau behind him, and then he took her arm and helped her to her feet and held her lightly while he rummaged under the cushion. His arm was comfortingly strong: it never gave an inch as she clung to it, but was like a rock under her frozen fingers.

"There! That's it!" he said after a moment, replacing the cushion for her to sit down again. "Wait before you sit yourself down so that I can wrap the rug round you. If you sit in it, like, you'll find the wind won't cut through so much."

She let him drape it round her and sat back in it as he told her, reveling in its warmth. This indeed was real luxury, to have such a thick rug to snuggle into: why, it was even warmer than Uncle Ebenezer's sacks! She thanked him gratefully, but the silent James had said his say, and returned to the top of the portmanteau with her hold-all in his hands.

"Let me take that again," she said, but he told her gruffly that it was best where it was.

"It ain't all that heavy," he said. "Let it bide."

So they travelled on over the miles from Windover station to the Manor and Windover village, James not uttering another word and Polly too timid to start a conversation, and, being warmer now, she was free to listen to the snatches of talk that were blown back to them from the box, shouted above the wind.

"So you'm left Oxford, Mr. Charles," said Peters, after he had related the histories of the horses that had come and gone at the Manor since Mr. Harroby's last visit. "That's a fine old city, now, ain't it? I remember I stopped there with an uncle of mine what ran a stables in the old days, and a fine thing he made of it too, letting out hacks to the young gentlemen. But them clocks, now, don't they keep you awake at night? I never could get used to 'em, ding-dong all over the town every quarter of an hour, and all just a minute or so after each other. . . . I reckon there wasn't a minute of the day or night when some clock wasn't telling of the time. You couldn't miss a train by not knowing the time in Oxford, now, could you?"

Charles laughed and said that he had got used to it. "And I'm afraid it's made me no more punctual in my habits than I've always been," he added.

"They tell me as you're going to be a clergyman, Mr. Charles," went on old Peters curiously, and the young man laughed again more ruefully.

"Sir John has paid for my education all these years on the understanding that I go into the Church," he said. "I've tried to impress on him that I'm not cut out for it— I've not got enough of the Chrisitan spirit in me, Peters!—but he only says it's a lot of nonsense, and that there's always been a Harroby at Windover Rectory and I'm the only one of the family that's the right age for it when the Reverend Lionel goes. . . . And then, you see, my mother cried—and she's a widow, of course, with six other children to provide for—and so I could do nothing else but agree to do what the Squire wished. But it goes sadly against the grain, Peters, it does indeed."

"It would be nice to hev you at the Rectory all the same, Mr. Charles," said Peters. "And you'd have room enough there for your mother and all your brothers and sisters, wouldn't you? It's a fine big house, is the Rectory."

"As to its accommodation I believe it would take a family three times the size of ours," said Mr. Harroby drily. "There are thirty bedrooms, I've been told, not counting the attics. But I've a feeling, Peters, that her ladyship will expect to see my sermons before I mount the pulpit on a Sunday, and that wouldn't suit my book at all."

"Well, it takes an eddicated gentleman like yourself to preach sermons, of course," said Peters consolingly. "The Rector, the Reverend Lionel, he do preach the mos' beautiful sermons, Mr. Charles. Mind you, I can't say as any of us properly understands 'em like, but her ladyship she do say they're second to none, and she ought to know; while as fur Sir John, he spreads his handkerchief over his head and sleeps like a babby all the way through. 'Tis beautiful the way the Rector's words do flow along. Latin and Greek, it's all of a piece with him, as I dessay it might be with yourself, Mr. Charles. When the Rector gets up into that there pulpit of his he puts his watch down alongside of his book and for three-quarters of an hour he never wants for a word. It's just like as if he were wound up with his watch, sir."

"Ten minutes will be my limit," said Charles. "But then, you see, I've no vocation for it. There were men up at Oxford with me who liked nothing better than a chance to get up on their feet and preach, but, feeling as I do about it, that I've been persuaded into the business against my will, it is just an impertinence for me to tell other people what they ought to do. . . . I don't know enough about life, and I don't care enough for it, and that's what it is. It's nothing but a mockery, Peters, and there's a saying somewhere in the Bible that God is not mocked, and that is a saying that I do most sincerely believe. But no argument will budge the Providence that rules my life, and so I must just say that Squire's will be done, and leave it like that. In due course the old gentleman will have another Harroby at Windover Rectory, and I dare say I shall have all the shooting and hunting I can wish for in exchange for my indifferent sermons. Most of my friends would say it was a good bargain, as good as any I could wish for, situated as I am."

They breasted a hill and an icy rain was blowing now in the wind, and suddenly the young man reined in the horses and drew the carriage to a halt.

"What about that girl in the back?" he said. "Won't she get soaked? . . . James, get out a rug or something and give it to her, will you?"

"I already have, sir," said James, and Peters said he hoped it wasn't the best one, as there was an old one she could have rather than spoil her ladyship's.

"James can dry it off in front of your harness-room

fire," said Charles consolingly. "It's the snuggest place at the Manor, that harness-room of yours, Peters, and I'm glad James used his head. It's a scullery-maid we're hoping to bring Cook, after all, not a block of ice. She can get that from the fishmonger!"

And with that he touched the horses with the whip and they moved on, but there was not quite so much comfort in the warm rug now that Polly knew that it belonged to Lady Augusta, and she could not enjoy it any more. She felt she had no right to such luxury, and James had been wrong to let her revel in it as she had. The thin old rug would have been good enough for her, just as Aunt Hannah's thin old clothes were good enough to be made over for her. Humbly Polly knew that Aunt Hannah and Peters had the right ideas about her and her station, and it did not comfort her to know that James sat glum and silent and resentful for the rest of the way.

Thinking about Aunt Hannah, and the kind but firm way in which she had taken charge of her, she found herself wondering if the Squire and Lady Augusta had taken Mr. Charles's future in hand as firmly and relentlessly. She had always thought that rich people did not have to make uncomfortable decisions: she had imagined, from what her aunts told her, that the gentry naturally enjoyed themselves all their lives, with big houses to live in and servants to wait on them and horses to ride and carriages to drive about in and good food to eat. . . . But now it seemed, from the scraps of conversation she had overheard between Mr. Charles and the old groom, that even the gentry could be unhappy and have to do things they did not want to do. . . .

The rain and the cold gradually grew less about her and she slept, and woke to find an arm being removed rather roughly from her shoulders, and the lights from many windows streaming out into the sweep of a carriage drive.

With a careless word of thanks to old Peters, Charles Harroby handed him the reins and swung himself down, and Polly heard a girl's voice saying: "Charles! At last! . . . Are you frozen quite?" before the warmth of the big doorway took his tall figure from her sight.

The wagonette moved on into the stable yard and after young Mr. Harroby's luggage had been unloaded at a side door, where it was received by a footman and a boy in buttons, Polly was helped down and conducted by James to another door, leading directly into the kitchen.

As he took up her hold-all easily in one hand, he glanced at her again and wondered if she really could be as much as nearly fourteen. She did not look half that age with the rug gone from her black jacket, and the gray skirt that had obviously belonged to somebody much larger trailing on the wet cobbles of the yard. Her corn-colored hair under the battered hat had almost escaped its pins by this time and was half-way down her back, and in the light of the windows she looked small and frightened, and it was a look that suddenly pierced his heart. She was much too young to put up a fight against that wicked old bully of a cook.

He took her cold little hand gently in his spare one and drew her towards the closed back door.

"Don't be scared," he said in a low voice. "Always remember there's kind folk as well as unkind in the world, and for one as scolds there'll be two or three that will speak you well."

It was a long speech for him to make, and it comforted her and warmed her more than her ladyship's rug had done. She thanked him quickly and shyly, and he dropped her hand and opened the back door. And then he left her to make her way inside it alone.

3

AT first sight Polly thought that the kitchen at Windover Manor must be the largest in the world: she could not imagine that Buckingham Palace had one larger.

The cooking range alone was longer than her Uncle Reuben's cottage, taking it from front to back, though not quite as high, and there were enough ovens in it to bewilder anyone. The kitchen floor seemed to be composed of big square flagstones, which Polly was to get to know very well during the weeks that followed, because one of her duties was to help the other kitchen-maid, Annie, to scrub them over every afternoon.

Beyond the kitchen, down two steps, was an enormous scullery, with several stone sinks in it and a pump at the far end. There were very few water taps in the Manor, and although Lady Augusta had talked about having a bathroom put in Sir John set his face against it and would not be budged. The water situation was bad enough in a dry summer, he said, especially when the house was full of guests, without having a wasteful bathroom to run off the precious stuff. The two wells that supplied the house, though deep, had been known to run almost dry at times, and, after all, there were plenty of tubs and plenty of housemaids to take them round to the bedrooms in the mornings. And what could be nicer, asked the Squire, or more luxurious if it came to that, than a bath in your own dressing-room in front of a good fire?

The only bathrooms the Squire had encountered on his visits to his friends' houses were icy, vast apartments, with nothing but tepid water in the brass taps, and large grates in which sulky fires refused to draw.

The duties of a housemaid in a house the size of the

Manor were at that time unknown to Polly. There seemed to be a great number of upper servants in the house, because one of her tasks was to help wait on them at their meals in the servants' hall, but none of them took any notice of her. Some of them she scarcely ever saw, because Mr. Harris and Mr. Everitt, and the Squire's valet Mr. Finch, and her ladyship's lady's maid Miss Edwards, all had their breakfast in the housekeeper's room with Mrs. Grim, and were waited on there by the still-room maid, Mary.

During those first weeks it was only her companion in misfortune, Annie, who made their joint slavery under Cook bearable. At first she thought she never would learn to find her way down to the kitchen on her own, and if she left the temporary safety of her remote attic she felt she would get hopelessly lost in the passages and staircases that confronted her, especially at half past four of a winter's morning, when all the light she had was the guttering piece of candle in her bedroom candlestick. She was thankful when the rough but kindly Annie took her under her wing, and conducted her every morning down the several flights of stairs and bare corridors to the kitchens, where their labors lay. The carpeted passages and stair cases ended on the other side of the baize doors that separated the servants' quarters from the rest of the house, and once down the final flight of back stairs a long, stone-floored passage lay to the right, with a long line of bells, each with its separate name-plate beneath it, hanging above. This passage led to the servants' hall and kitchens, as directly as sundry corners and steps up and down could make it.

The first door on the right at the bottom of the stairs was that belonging to the housekeeper's room, which was cozily carpeted, as Polly noticed one day when the door was open as she went by. It had a piano in one corner, chiefly used for standing Mrs. Grim's family photographs on, and a round table covered by a blue serge cloth. An aspidistra in a pink china jardinière stood in one of the windows, and a small bamboo table, similarly draped in blue serge and covered with knick-knacks, stood in the other. Blue serge curtains were at the windows, and more of it draped the mantelpiece, over which was a picture of the Queen, taken in her Golden Jubilee year. This picture was flanked on either side by faded photographs of the Squire's father driving a four-in-hand, and his coachman on the box of an old-fashioned barouche-landau. On the shelf there was a further assortment of Mrs. Grim's treasures, such as boxes ornamented with sea-shells, and a china pig with a pincushion in its back, and a black marble clock, and a Japanese fan, and below them a copper kettle sang away merrily on the hob.

Next to the housekeeper's room was the still-room, ruled over by Mary, who had the lightest hand with cakes for many a mile round. From this room there always came pleasant smells of cooking cakes, especially at tea-time, when trays would issue forth in the hands of the footmen, laden with sandwiches and scones and tiny iced cakes.

Beyond the still-room was the butler's pantry, usually the scene of much activity, as Mr. Harris believed in driving his young footmen, and then came the boot-room, where the boy in buttons polished boots and cleaned knives on a knife-board under the constant surveillance of Mr. Everitt, who cuffed his head for no reason, and handed on the butler's discipline in a somewhat modified form.

Between this room and the servants' hall was the lamp-room, where old Burke—who was James's uncle and brother to his father, the head gamekeeper—collected every lamp in the house every morning and trimmed and filled it and polished the chimney before taking it back to where it belonged. There were fifty-six rooms in the Manor, and some of them had no less than half a dozen lamps, because the luxury of gas had not yet come to Windover, and there were more than twenty in the hall and porch and stairs, so that the old man's lair smelt perpetually of paraffin.

Next to this rather smelly room there was the servants' hall, with a long table for meals, and about twenty chairs round it, and armchairs round the fire where Cook liked to take her nap in the afternoons, and beyond this again, various pantries and larders, stone-floored and with slate shelves, which housed baskets of eggs, and great jugs of milk, and crocks of cream, as yellow as the butter that waited beside it for the wooden pats that would mold it into shape. Whole cheeses stood there on the shelves, too, and bins full of flour, and joints of meat and hams hung from hooks in the ceiling. The game larder was outside, with doors and windows of wire mesh, that let the wind blow through the birds and the hares that were strung up there.

The kitchen-maids had their midday meal at half past two, long after the dining-room lunch was finished and the servants' dinner done with and washed up. Then, before Cook settled down to her nap, Polly and her stable companion were set down at the kitchen table in front of plates of left-overs and told to eat it up and be quick about it, or they would never get the floor scrubbed and dry before tea. The left-overs were a great deal better than any of the meals that Polly had been accustomed to at home, if rather tepid by that time, and being famished she was glad to eat everything on her plate before taking her pail and starting to scrub.

But as the days went by and her bewilderment grew less, and the kitchens assumed a size in proportion with the rest of the house—though to be sure she never put her nose through any of the baize doors that shut her in, and had no notion of what was on the other side of them—she became conscious only of raw hands, aching back and legs, and a desire to get out of Cook's way before she started shouting at her. Cook was so made that it was imperative for her to have somebody to bully, and she usually picked on the smallest and weakest of the servants for that purpose.

The black-leading of the vast range in the darkness of the early morning under Annie's directions, the feverish attempt to get it to light without filling the kitchen with smoke, and terror of Cook's fury if she should have to come down to a sulky fire and lukewarm kettles, petrified the poor child into speechless misery. This was nothing, however, to the mountains of vegetables that were brought to the back door by the head gardener, old Graves: there seemed to be more in one morning than could be sold in Aunt Hannah's shop in a week. The waste of food, too, appalled her.

"All this lovely fresh bread," she mourned as she helped Annie to wash the dishes. "All thrown away. . . . Whatever happens to it all, Annie?"

"It goes into the swill for the Squire's pigs, of course," said Annie, sniffling over her bowl of water. She suffered from perpetual colds throughout the winter.

"The Squire's pigs?" Polly's eyes grew round. "Is he a farmer, then?"

"Lor' bless you, no!" said Annie good-humoredly. "It's the home farm, you duffer. All big houses like this have their own home farms. How else would we have enough milk and cream and butter and eggs, and such?"

Polly said no more, though she puzzled over it in silence. There was Sir John and Lady Augusta and the two young ladies, and round these four people the Manor, its servants, gardens, and farm, revolved. There were rooms to be cleaned every day, hundreds of lamps filled and cleaned, bedroom candlesticks to be polished, great joints of meat roasted, and game and chickens such as she had never dreamed of in her short life, with their accompanying sauces and vegetables, and all just so that these four people should not find a speck of dust if they went into one of the many rooms, or a lamp that was un-lighted—though they might never go near it—and always have a dinner set in front of them fit for the Queen her-self.

It never occurred to Polly in those first weeks, incarcerated as she was in the big scullery, her aching hands washing ice out of Brussels sprouts and peeling potatoes and scrubbing carrots and celery, while she wept over strings of onions, that the Squire and his wife and daugh-ters were very seldom alone in their dining-room and their large rooms. Dinner and luncheon parties to Polly were just occasions for even larger mountains of vegetables, and even more violent scolding from Cook.

"Are you going to be all night with them leeks, Polly?

For 'evin's sake, Annie, give the girl a 'and with them. She'll be hours yet, stoopid creetur ... and where's them onions for my sauce? Didn't I *tell* you to do them first?"

So it went on, while the days flew by and Polly's back never stopped aching, and her chilblained hands caused Cook to break forth again and even to resort to violence.

Polly never saw anybody from the other side of the baize doors. The scullery windows were painted over, so that the kitchen-maids could not look out and waste their time, although outside them there was only a very small herb-garden with the blank wall of one of the stables beyond it.

She knew, because she heard his name as she was serving the vegetables to the upper servants, that Mr. Charles was still at the Manor, but she never saw him. She got up at four and worked through the day in kitchen and scullery until she crept off to bed, dropping with weariness, when the last saucepan had been scoured and dried and put away at half past ten or eleven at night.

And except for the silent James, who sometimes came to the back door with a message, and stood there waiting for an answer and staring at her without uttering a word, the world outside that contained her relatives, and the Squire, and his family, was as far away from her as if she had been shut up in a dungeon to which Cook, as gaoler, held the key.

Charles Harroby enjoyed his stay at the Manor because it was in his nature to enjoy life, and above everything he enjoyed shooting the Squire's game and riding his horses, which were far better than any his mother could afford.

Of the two girls he liked Josey best. She was the one nearer to his own age, being only two years older than he was, and there was a lot of common sense in her, accompanied by a wicked sense of humor akin to his own. She sat a horse, too, better than any other woman in the county, and followed the hounds with her father every time he went out. Lady Augusta was old-fashioned enough to disapprove of her daughters hunting: in her young days it had been considered fast, and no lady would have dreamt of doing more than riding to a meet in her carriage. But Josey had tastes that often horrified her mother, so that from time to time, after she had expressed some particularly outrageous desire, Lady Augusta felt forced to request her father to remonstrate with her.

"I detest the habit of smoking, even in a man, as you well know, John," she said once. "But in a woman it is abominable, and in the lowest possible taste. I do not mind how many society women indulge in the practice: I will not have one of our daughters gaining a reputation for being fast!"

"If I were sure that Josey smoked only out of bravado, my dear, I would be the first to agree with you," Sir John replied. "But she enjoys a cigarette, nauseating as you may find it, and, as long as she indulges in her taste for tobacco in private, I cannot see that any great harm will be done to her reputation!"

"In private!" exclaimed Lady Augusta. "And, pray, how do you suggest that she should do that? I hope you are not intending her to smoke in her *bedroom*, John? For a young lady's bedroom to smell of tobacco would be quite dreadful."

"Of course I didn't mean that," said Josey's father, smiling. "I'm sure Josey herself would be equally fastidious in that direction. No, what I meant was that when we have no guests in the house I see no reason why Josey should not join me in the smoking-room sometimes of an evening, and enjoy her cigarette-smoking there."

The fact was that Josey, for all her ugly little monkeyish face and boyish ways, was her father's favorite: there was a warmth about her that his stately elder daughter completely lacked.

Ellen took after her mother and had only once exhibited any depth of feeling, when at the age of eighteen, she had fallen in love with the son of a neighboring farmer. Fortunately Lady Augusta was soon able to rout the undesirable young man and to scold her daughter into obedience and outward docility, removing her to the Continent for some months so that she might forget her hobbledehoy in the company of those of the Fanes who were either taking the cure at Baden, or enjoying the pleasures of the south of France in their sober English fasion.

Whether Ellen forgot the young man was never known, because she never mentioned him after they returned home, but it was quite certain that he forgot her, because he married in the following summer a young woman who, being a farmer's daughter, was of his own station in life, and no doubt a great deal more suitable.

For the next ten years Ellen had held herself aloof from suitors, although to be sure she had not very many, most men being put off from the start by her coolness and chilling dignity. Just before Charles came to visit his cousins in the January of 1889, however, something had happened that had set the whole neighborhood talking, because old Lady Eleanor Fane died and left her considerable fortune to Ellen Harroby, to be paid to her, so the will ran, "on the day of her marriage."

The fact was that the news of Ellen's unhappy love affair had filtered through to her great-aunt over the Fane family grapevine some years previously, with several important parts left out, and being deaf and hearing only the half of it, and imagining that it was want of money that was the stumbling block, and being sorry for the Squire's daughters because she had never liked her niece Augusta, the old lady had immediately made a will leaving all that she had to Ellen, with a proviso that seemed sensible when she made it, and now that she was dead, ten years later, only looked as if she had been making game of that aloof young woman from the grave.

"You will find, Charles," said Sir John when he was discussing it one night over a glass of port when they were alone together, "you will find that a lot of people make that kind of mistake. They will put off rectifying some item in their wills, thinking that there is plenty of time; and the years go by, and suddenly they die, leaving things in a muddle. But there is no need for Ellen to be hurt, and I fancy she knows it, although she has never mentioned it to me. It was a kindly act, kindly meant, and I have no fear that it will be likely to lay her open to fortune-hunters. She is a very sensible young woman."

"It seems a bit unfair on Josey," said Charles.

"Ah, Josey!" The Squire's eyes were suddenly tender. "But she does not resent it either, Charles."

"Josey would resent nothing," said Charles warmly. "I should not say there was a pennyworth of jealousy in her."

The Squire was silent for a moment and then he observed quietly that Josey would not be without her portion when he was gone. It had occurred to him more than once lately how happy he would be if in the future Charles were to settle down at Windover Rectory with Josey for his wife. The living there would not be vacant until the Reverend Lionel gave it up, and he had signalled his desire to do this in about four years' time, when he would reach the age of eighty. Charles, in the meantime, had diffidently broached the subject of his ordination, which was to be at Easter, by mentioning the invitation he had received from an Oxford friend to help him in the large East End parish where he was now a priest.

Charles had always been an admirer of the vigorous young Raymond Latimer, and he thought he would like to join him in his efforts, and Sir John could see nothing but good coming from such an association. The work would be hard and unrewarding, and there would be no time to play, which would mean that when the time came for him to step into his old cousin's shoes in sleepy little Windover, Charles would be more than ready to oblige.

The good Squire had no idea of the radical notions that his protégé had picked up during his sojourn at Oxford, nor of the extreme Socialistic leanings of his friend, Mr. Latimer, otherwise he might have persuaded Lionel to retire right away, leaving the Rectory open for Charles and his mother.

In the Squire's view a great many young men would give their eyes for a living like Windover. The income was at least five hundred pounds a year, and it would be his for life. With the help of his mother's income before he married, and assistance from the Manor if Josey became his wife, Charles could have his hunting and keep a couple of carriages, and as many servants as he needed down at the Rectory. Sir John would see that his brothers and sisters were provided for: he had already spoken to a friend at the Foreign Office about the second boy, the third being destined for the Navy, while the girls, young as they were, were so pretty that he had no doubt they would soon find husbands when they were out of the schoolroom.

So the Squire sipped his port and dreamed his dreams, while Charles sat opposite him, outwardly acquiescent, but frowning a little as he twirled the stem of his wineglass in his fingers, thinking that nothing would induce him to become Rector at Windover under the eye of his cousin's wife, Lady Augusta, while of Josey he did not think at all.

On the morning following this conversation the hunt was meeting at Broughton Park, and James came up early to the stables, cutting through the lower vegetable garden to get there quickly. As he skirted the rows of kale and cabbages that were frozen into the ground he suddenly heard the sound of stifled sobbing coming from the potting-shed by the gate.

Startled out of his wits, he stopped and looked round, and then, through the half-open door of the shed, he caught sight of a cap and apron.

He retraced his steps unwillingly, being a lad who liked to mind his own business: he was speechless enough without the added embarrassment of having to deal with a woman's tears, and yet he was too kind-hearted to pass by without taking any notice. He looked inside the shed and saw Polly, weeping into her apron and oblivious of everything except the present misery of her life under Cook, and as he guessed the cause for such abandoned weeping his heart was filled with pity for her, and fury against the old harridan who had hurt her. But, although he would have liked to go into the Manor kitchen and brain the woman with one of her own rolling-pins, all he could do was to stand and stare, and shift from one foot to the other, and stammer out miserably, "Is anything the matter, Polly, my dear?"

Which was a ridiculous thing to say on the face of it,

because it was obvious that something was the matter, or she would not have chosen the cold potting-shed to weep in on the last morning in January.

She looked up with a small gasp of fright at the sound of his voice, and he marked the thinness of her arms, and her swollen, bleeding hands, and the ugly bruise that was coming up on her cheekbone.

"What has happened to your face?" he asked, more gently still, and she put up her hand quickly to cover it and tried to smile at him through her tears. He was so large and comforting that the very sight of him was consoling.

"It's nothing, thank you, James," she said. "That is ... Cook boxed my ears, and I dare say I deserved it. . . . It was the carrots, you see. I hadn't looked in the basket to see if they were there when Mr. Graves came with the vegetables this morning, and she was angry. . . . I came running out to find him, but he isn't anywhere about, and I dursn't go back without telling him. Cook will murder me if I do." She gave a hiccupping sigh and a tear slid down her bruised cheek. "It's nothing, though, James ... don't give it a thought. I'll get used to it, I expect ... Annie says I will, given time. But a month has gone already and it has seemed all of two years. . . ."

"She's no right to hit you." James's voice was deep and rumbling with emotion. "You're too small for that hard work ... I thought you was when I first saw you. You'd have every right to run home, and nobody could blame you for it."

"Oh no, I couldn't do that!" Polly's eyes were shocked. "I wouldn't have a character if I ran away, and what would my Auntie Ada do without my money? She's coming to fetch it when the month is up tomorrow: my Uncle Ebenezer is bringing her along in his van, and it would be dreadful if she came and found no five shillings because I'd run home."

James was perplexed for her, seeing the full size of the problem, and then his face brightened.

"I'll speak to my mother, what's a friend of Mrs. Grim's," he said. "I'll ask her to go and see her and tell her that you're not happy, and see if she can't move you to be a housemaid. The work wouldn't be so hard, seeing as you are so little and so thin."

"But I'm strong," said Polly quickly. "And I wouldn't like Mrs. Grim to think I was complaining. . . ."

"She won't think that. Not the way my mother puts it," said James stoutly. "And seeing as your auntie lives so far away, maybe you'd be able to come to our house on your evening out sometimes. You'd be kindly welcome, I'm sure."

"Oh, thank you, James." Polly was breathless with gratitude, and her tear-stained face beamed at him. Cook was momentarily forgotten, and when he told her that he would find some carrots himself and bring them to the back door before he saw to the horses, her happiness was complete. She ran back to the kitchen with her tears dried by the wind, singing softly as she went. It was the first time she had felt like singing since she had come to the Manor.

James was as good as his word, and the next afternoon his mother called up to see Mrs. Grim with a pot of quince jam. Mabel Burke had once been still-room maid there, and Mrs. Grim always said she had never had one since who could make quince jam like Mabel's. She made her kindly welcome and poked the fire so that it blazed up cheerfully.

"I was just about to have my tea," said Mrs. Grim. "I'll ring the bell and tell Mary to get another cup for you, dear, and some more of her scones. She can't touch you for jams and jellies, Mabel, but she has a very light hand with cakes and pastries, and her scones are second to none."

The tea was replenished and the two old friends settled down comfortably by the fire on the cold winter afternoon, and presently, as she sipped her tea, and after she had praised the scones, Mabel told the housekeeper her errand.

"It's that great soft lad of mine that sent me long to see you, Mrs. Grim," she said apologetically. "You know what he's like. He can't bear what he calls seeing people put upon, and so he asked me to speak to you. 'If you think I'm going to teach Mrs. Grim her business, my dear,' I said, 'you're very much mistaken.' I wasn't still-room maid under you for five years without knowing you can manage your own affairs, ma'am, and that's the truth of it."

Mrs. Grim's small black eyes grew suddenly sharp, and the smile faded from her face.

"What does James want?" she asked.

"Well, it was this way. You know that yesterday there was that big meet out at Broughton? Well, James had to be out early with the horses, and he was cutting through the lower vegetable garden to the stables when he came upon the new kitchen-maid in the potting-shed, crying her eyes out."

"In the *potting-shed?*" Mrs. Grim sounded scandalized. "Whatever was she doing there?"

"I don't know. I couldn't make head nor tail of it. But there'd been a fuss about some carrots and your cook had been laying about her. James said she had a great black bruise on her face, and he says that everyone knows that your cook has got a most shocking temper."

"Well yes, she is a bad-tempered woman," agreed Mrs. Grim unwillingly.

"James was quite upset," went on Mabel. "He says he thinks the girl is too small for such hard work ... but I told him you'd know best, of course, Mrs. Grim; and, I said, seeing as the child is so far from home I'd have no objection if she came to us when she has her night off in the month. It might make her less homesick."

"*Evening* off," corrected Mrs. Grim with asperity. "And she must be in by nine, prompt."

"My James will see her home," said Mrs. Burke. "He's a steady lad, is James. You could trust your own daughter to him, ma'am, if you had one."

"Which I haven't, thank God," snapped Mrs. Grim. "Girls is more trouble than they're worth." She frowned into the fire, relapsing into offended silence. The truth was that her conscience was troubling her a little, and she thought of Polly with some compunction. The kitchen work wasn't really fit for her: she was a little scrap of a thing, and there was Annie's younger sister Nellie, who at twelve years old would have made two of Polly. She was a great strapping girl, and wanting a place, although the housekeeper did not like taking them so young, and did not approve of putting sisters to the same work. Yet it did seem that it might be better to let Annie have her sister there in the kitchen, and train Polly for a housemaid instead. They could always do with young housemaids at the Manor: the upper housemaids were for ever leaving to get married or to better themselves—whatever that might mean, because they would find few places as good as those at the Manor.

After Mabel had gone Mrs. Grim got up and went out of the room, smoothing down her black alpaca apron over her plain black silk, the keys on the ribbon at her waist jingling a little as she walked, and her underskirt rustling as much as her ladyship's.

Down she went, along the stone corridor under the rows of bells, past the butler's pantry where Mr. Harris was busy decanting old crusted port wine—a difficult operation that he performed with great skill—past the lamp-room where Burke was still busy with his lamps, past all the pantries and the larders and the china-closets, past the servants' hall where Cook sat snoring loudly by the fire, an empty tumbler beside her on the table, and came at last to the kitchen and the two girls who knelt there, scrubbing and scouring and wiping dirty suds away into their buckets.

"Good afternoon, Polly. Good afternoon, Annie," said Mrs. Grim graciously.

"Good afternoon, ma'am," chorused the girls respectfully and then, as Annie sat back on her heels while Polly would have scrambled up, she motioned to them to go on with their work.

"You've got a nasty bruise on your face, Polly, my dear," she observed mildly. "How did you manage to get that?"

Polly was tongue-tied, and it was Annie who hastily answered for her.

"You caught it on the pump-handle yesterday morning, didn't you, Polly?" she said. "Bruised it something shocking, hasn't she, ma'am?"

"She has bruised it, certainly," said Mrs. Grim coldly. "When you have finished your work here, Polly, I will be obliged if you will come to my room for some embrocation to put on it. It will take down the swelling."

She turned on her heel and left them and went back to her room, and the girls hurried over their work so that Polly could go.

"My mother says there's nothing like raw steak for a bruise," said Annie. "You want to nip into the larder and cut off a bit."

"And get another box on the ears for doing it, I suppose?" said Polly. "No thank you. I'd rather have the embrocation."

"Imbrocation is what they use for hosses' legs," said Annie. "And though we may work like a hoss we ain't hosses yet, are we?"

But Polly only laughed, and went to empty her bucket in the yard. It was just five o'clock when, washed and tidied, she knocked timidly on the housekeeper's door and was told to come in.

Mrs. Grim greeted her kindly enough.

"Come and sit down by the fire, Polly," she said. "Mary's made you some toast, and there is a pot of honey that my nephew sent me in that corner cupboard. Get it out, child, and have some with the toast."

Polly saw to her astonishment that a table set out for one was placed by the fire, and she was overwhelmed to discover that she was expected to eat her tea there, under the eye of the august Mrs. Grim, and in fact she would have been almost less nervous had she been asked to take tea under the eye of the Queen.

But Mrs. Grim seemed to be a much friendlier and nicer person behind her own door, and she made enquiries about the work she was doing, and how she liked it, and found some arnica for her bruised face, and tincture of iodine for her chilblained hands.

"Your aunt came this morning for your money," she said. "She asked how you were getting on, but she could not stay to see you because Mr. Phillips could not wait long, and because her youngest child has been taken ill with typhoid fever. I told her she should send him to the hospital, as there are the other children to consider and they might take it from him, but she wouldn't hear of it."

"If he were in the hospital in Windover I could go and see him on my evening out," said Polly. "He is a dear little boy, is Sam, and he always loved me best."

"The hospital in Windover?" Mrs. Grim frowned. "There's no hospital here, my dear!"

"Oh, but there must be!" Polly's eyes grew round with surprise. "There's a girl comes to the back door every night for two score of eggs and a jug of milk and some butter that Cook has ready for her, and when I asked Annie where she was taking them, she said to the hospital."

"Indeed?" Mrs. Grim's tone was dry. "So that's where our butter and eggs are going. . . ."

"Yes, ma'am. Annie said—"

"Never mind what Annie says!" Mrs. Grim smiled unwillingly. "That girl tells more lies on the spur of the moment than any I've had, but she's a hard worker and a willing one, and for that I am prepared to overlook such failings. . . . Well, my dear, drink up your tea and tell me if you think you would like to be a housemaid here, instead of working in the kitchen? It's hard, mind, equally as hard as kitchen work, but there wouldn't be all that scrubbing and peeling of vegetables, and your hands wouldn't break out as they do now. I'll bind those up for you before you go."

The joy of getting away from Cook's domination was almost too much. For such an opportunity Polly felt she would have helped old Burke with his lamps, or the bootboy with his boots and knife-cleaning. Nothing would have been too hard as long as she could escape from Cook.

Mrs. Grim sent her back to the kitchen with an admonition to hold her tongue, and the next morning she was sent to report to the under-housemaid, Doris, and learn from her how to do a grate on the other side of the baize doors.

About the middle of February, when the days were getting longer and the snowdrops were white carpets on either side of the avenue, Cook suddenly departed, and another kinder, good-tempered person took her place.

But Polly saw little of her, except at meals in the servants' hall, which she now took with the other servants, waited on by Annie and her sister. And one evening in every month she went down to Mrs. Burke's cottage, and was welcomed there kindly by the head gamekeeper and his wife, and treated as one of the family, and when it was time for her to go James walked back with her through the unlighted lanes.

But in spite of his quiet ways she found him a very companionable person, and he taught her a great deal about the birds and the plants in the neighborhood, so that soon she could recognize the bird-calls for herself, and knew the name of nearly every wild flower in the hedges near his home. It was, in fact, like having an elder brother about the place, and now that she was happy and contented her arms grew less thin, and she began to fill the dresses that had been too large for her, and her face grew rosier and prettier, so that whenever he looked at her James's diffidence increased, and his mother told her that she was a sight for sore eyes.

The years passed, and Polly's wages were increased to ten shillings a month, and now she was allowed one whole afternoon and evening out in a fortnight, as well as most Sunday evenings. She was able to pay her train fare from Windover to Market Broughton, and leave some money with her Aunt Phillips for her sister Ada to collect on the following market-day, and she shot up into a radiant young creature, with her corn-colored hair dressed neatly and trim dresses made to fit Polly Kettle, and not handed down to her from somebody else.

And as she began to stand on her own feet and was able to wonder and laugh at herself for being so silly and frightened when she first came to Windover, which now seemed to be her second home, up in London Charles Harroby became Curate in the large London parish where Raymond Latimer was now Vicar, and was learning, not easily, how ordinary working people faced starvation and illness and privation and despair.

Both in their separate ways were learning: Polly about the class much above her own, and how it lived and thought and talked, and Charles about the class so much below his own, and the courage with which it faced its difficulties, until in the year 1893 their lives, that had once touched briefly at Windover railway station and swung apart, to travel on parallel lines for four years, now suddenly swung together disastrously, bringing trouble to them both.

The Squire died in Polly's third year at the Manor, and just before Easter in the following year the Rector, Lionel Harroby, died of a heart attack on the morning of Good Friday. Lady Augusta telegraphed at once to Charles to leave his parish and come to take up his duties at Windover, as curate-in-charge until he could be appointed as the new Rector.

Old Peters had been pensioned off at Christmas and lived now in one of the almshouses in the village, and it was James who brought the dog-cart down to the station that April afternoon to meet Charles. At twenty-two James was a young giant, and, although not quite as speechless as in the old days, he had a gentle, diffident way with him, as if he were afraid he might do damage because of his strength.

He had Charles's luggage up in the back of the cart in a few minutes, and sat beside him while he took the spirited little horse out of the station yard, but beyond commenting on the countryside, which was looking very lovely just then, Charles said little, and James needed no encouragement to relapse into his former silence.

The fact was that Charles had come to Windover in a militant mood. He was far from imagining that the life of

an East End parish would give him the satisfaction that it
gave his friend Latimer, but he was equally sure that
nothing on earth would make him settle down for life at
Windover, under the eye of Lady Augusta.

4

THE whole of the attic floor at the Manor was given over to the servants. The floors of the rooms were scrubbed white, a few pieces of old carpet being laid by the beds, not for comfort, but in case of splinters. A splinter in an unwashed foot could cause a great deal of inconvenience to the people on whose errands the foot ran.

The bedsteads were of iron, with overlay mattresses that felt as if they were made of iron too. Cook was the only one who had a feather bed to keep her cozy on winter nights when the attics were too near the stars for comfort, but then Cook had kitchen-maids to work for her while she lay abed. And of course, on the floor below, in her bedroom next to the sewing-room, Mrs. Grim had a feather bed too, as well as sundry other luxuries like oatmeal soap and damask towels, that the attics never heard of, while Harris kept the menservants in order in the small, cold north rooms of the east wing. And what they and Mr. Harris slept on certainly none of the maidservants knew.

Lady Augusta cut down the number of her menservants on the death of the Squire. His valet Finch left a week after the funeral, and with him went Everitt, leaving the second footman Albert, and the hall-boy Sam, to manage under the direction of the butler and a parlor-maid, Emms, while a groom took the footman's place on the carriage when her ladyship drove out.

On the whole the maids' rooms at the Manor were more comfortable than any they had known in the crowded little cottages from which they came. The windows were small and high up under the eaves, but cottage windows were small too. Chests of drawers stood beneath them, so that there should not be the temptation to a young maid to idle away her time by standing gazing out at the village and the park when she was supposed to be making her bed or changing into her black afternoon dress, but then cottage windows were almost blocked up by chests of drawers, and crowded out by the number of beds that had to be accommodated in the rooms behind them.

There was space for plenty of furniture in the Manor attics, and each room had a chair with a cane seat, and a painted deal washstand, with a basin and jug of cold water, and there were cupboards in the walls—rather deep cupboards, with rows of pegs above, and velvety dust, smelling rather mousy, on the floorboards beneath.

There was of course no water-closet—there were but two in the whole house—and as regards bathing, in the smallest attic of all, on a square of linoleum, and midway between two doors and a window, a battered hip-bath stood for the convenience of the maids, with two large, brown-painted cans beside it. In these they might fetch hot and cold water up the three or four flights of stairs if they liked to take the trouble. During the summer the attics got very hot under the leaded roof, and Polly, who was now second under-housemaid, would bring a can of cold water upstairs overnight and splash about in the tin tub the next morning like a sparrow in a puddle.

Polly was eighteen that year, and had lately been given a large and rather stupid child to instruct in the ways of the Manor. This child's name was Winifred Dollis, and she was fourteen, fat, and adenoidal, and, as the head housemaid, Doris, tersely put it, as lazy as Hall's Dog.

But as this was her first place, and her mother was most anxious that she should stay and "be learnt in the ways of the gentry," Polly had taken her over from the head housemaid, and by dint of telling her things over and over again, and scolding her and laughing at the same time, and occasionally bullying her, got her into some sort of shape.

That particular May morning, when Polly got up as usual to have her cold bath at five o'clock, Winnie turned over in bed and groaned, and got out only after Polly,

coming back from her bath glowing from the cold water
and clad in a cotton chemise, pulled the clothes off her.

"How can you?" Winnie said, gazing at Polly with disgust. "And where did you get that chemise from? Wish I
had chemises with lace on 'em, like a lady. . . ."

"I made it myself," Polly said. "As you will be able to
one day, when your hands are cleaner. You never washed
last night before you went to bed, you dirty thing. The jug
is still standing in your basin, and there's a streak of black
over your eyebrow."

"What's the use of so much washing, when I'll only get
dirty again doing the grates?" demanded Winnie lazily.

"You can do what you like when you're at home," retorted Polly severely. "But here at the Manor you'll wash
if I have to come and scrub you myself. Go on, get up
quickly, Winnie dear, or we'll have Doris after us."

"Doris is still snoring her head off," said Winnie. "I can
hear her through this wall. . . . Wish I was a head housemaid and able to sleep as long as I liked. . . ."

"Wishing won't help nobody," said Polly good-humoredly. "And Doris didn't get to bed till after twelve last
night. Come on, hurry up, Winnie. And change those
stockings of yours for clean ones. They smell to high
heaven."

"I can't help it if my feet sweat," said Winnie. "And I
haven't got any more stockings. Those I was wearing yesterday had a great hole in them and Doris sent me up to
change 'em."

"And you only had these which you had never both-
ered to wash out?" Polly shook her head at her, smiling,
and picked up the offending stockings. "Come, if you
hurry up and get dressed I'll lend you a pair of mine, and
wash these out when we've done the grates. But we'll
never get them done if you don't get up now, dear." She
pulled open a drawer and took out a pair of black woollen
stockings that had turned slightly green with age, and
threw them to the grateful Winnie, and in a very little
while both girls were creeping down the back staircase
with their slippers and the bedroom candlesticks in their
hands. Old Burke saw to their candles, as well as those of

the family, and if they did not bring their candlesticks down in the morning they did not get new ones when the old were burnt out. Burke was mean about candles, and would seldom supply any until there was nothing but a puddle of grease left, with a curl of black wick lying in the middle.

He was already downstairs, opening the shutters of the servants' quarters. The girls hurried along the passage to a cupboard beyond the lamp-room and took from it a wooden housemaid's box full of brushes and emery paper and blacklead, and then, with Winnie staggering beneath a bucket of water and a large hessian cloth that was to be spread down in front of the hearths in their charge, they set out for the fireplaces that awaited them.

Polly liked the early mornings when the family was still asleep upstairs and nobody could hear her: it gave her a sense of belonging to the old house. So, she thought, must generations of girls have felt before her, as they laid fires and burnished fire-irons and dusted and swept and kept the big rooms shining and bright. This was where they belonged, as much as the family itself belonged. Without them the wheels would not turn, and the life of the whole Manor would come to a standstill.

Sometimes she tried to think what the house would be like with none of them there in the servants' hall, and it seemed to her that there would be a bleakness about it and an emptiness that no family would be able to endure. Take Lady Augusta, for instance, and the two young ladies—as they still called her daughters, though Miss Ellen was now thirty-two. Supposing—just supposing, because the thought was too fantastic to bear any relation to truth—that there was nobody to wait on them, to light their fires, to cook their food, to answer bells when they rang, to open doors for them, to wait up when they went out . . . why, it would seem as if the soul of the house had died.

Winnie dropped the steel fire-irons she was polishing with a clatter and recalled her to the job on hand.

"You must be quiet when you work, Winnie," Polly admonished her. "I've told you that again and again. Come along now . . . there's only the billiard-room left, and then you must get upstairs to her ladyship's dressing-room."

Winnie took up her hessian and the bucket again and Polly picked up the housemaid's box, and together they went on to the billiard-room, still smelling of the cigars that had been smoked in it the night before.

While Polly hurried to the big windows to draw the curtains and open the windows wide, Winnie, with the knowledge that this was the last grate downstairs to be done spurring her on, swept up the hearthrug in her arms so vigorously that something rolled out from under it and fell at her feet.

"Ooh!" she said, her eyes round with astonishment. "Look at that, Polly! A half-crown!"

"Don't touch it!" The gaiety went from Polly's face and her voice became suddenly peremptory. "Leave it be! It may have been put there of a purpose!"

"*Put* there?" Winnie goggled at her. "Whatever do you mean?"

"I mean this," said Polly, her pretty eyes dark with anger. "There's some among the gentry what likes to set traps for us girls in this way. Doris told me about it, when I was not more than you are now. They put money under the carpets, she said, making out they dropped it later, just to see if we're honest. It's a mean, dirty trick, and I've never seen it done here at the Manor before."

"But who would do it, then?" Winnie's astonishment was greater than her disapproval. "Her ladyship?"

"Good gracious, no! Of course not! Neither would Miss Josey, nor Miss Ellen . . . at least, I don't *think* Miss Ellen would! But I wouldn't put it past Mr. Crabb-Taylor, nor that friend of his."

"You mean Major Goodyer, with the shiny eyeglass?" Winnie nodded her head, old-fashioned. "They say in the village as he'll marry Miss Ellen. Do you think he will, Polly?"

Ellen Harroby had recently been paying a round of country-house visits with her sister, and had brought back the Crabb-Taylors and their friend Major Goodyer on a visit to the Manor. Mrs. Crabb-Taylor was a relative of

Lady Augusta's and welcomed because of it, but the welcome had not been extended quite so warmly to the gentlemen.

"*They* say? Who says?" said Polly scornfully. She put the half-crown on the chimney-piece and began to rub up the brass fender.

"Well, but do you think he will, Polly?"

"I shouldn't think so . . . she wouldn't have him."

"But she's ever so rich, isn't she, Polly? My auntie says she's got much more money than Miss Josey or her ladyship, and my auntie keeps the Post Office and ought to know."

"We all know what your auntie manages to discover down at the Post Office, thank you, Winnie! And it's common knowledge that Miss Ellen had a lot of money left to her, and what of it? It don't make her a fool, does it? If *we* can see what that Major Goodyer is after, surely she can, and if your auntie wants my opinion—" She stopped suddenly, aware that what she had been going to say was not the sort of thing to be passed on to Winnie's auntie at the Post Office. After all, what the Major's manservant, Mr. Giles, had to say to Mr. Harris, filtering through to the housemaids by way of Emms, and Mary in the still-room, was most likely only gossip, and spiteful at that. Mrs. Grim had always told Hannah Phillips in the old days, over those Sunday dinners above the greengrocery shop, that when a master got behind with the wages there was almost nothing he wasn't called by those that worked for him. And Polly disliked Mr. Giles fully as much as she disliked his master: he had a way of telling bawdy stories that sent the menservants into guffaws of laughter and the maids scurrying away with scarlet cheeks.

"Yes?" Winnie stopped in her work to stare at her. "What were you going to say, Polly?"

"I was going to say that if you don't hurry with that hearth you'll never reach her ladyship's dressing-room before Miss Edwards is ready to do the room," she said. "And before you go upstairs you'd better scrub your face. If Doris catches sight of you she'll recognize that black smudge as I did, and she's quite capable of taking you down into the yard and holding your head under the pump!"

She let Winnie go ahead of her while she straightened cushions and put the curtains right, and she was going to follow her young helper when she caught sight of the coin where she had left it on the chimney-piece. She stopped a minute thoughtfully, a feeling of resentment for the shabby trick played on them uppermost in her mind, and then her face brightened and her eyes sparkled with mischief.

"Findings keepings," her Uncle Reuben would say, but Aunt Ada would cap it with: "Never keep money though, dear, if you happen to find it—which I never have! Give it away at once if you want it to bring you luck, and then they do say it's the luckiest thing in the world. . . ."

Well, luck or no luck, she was going to teach somebody a lesson . . . .

She picked it up and went across the great hall and under the gallery to the little morning-room where Lady Augusta interviewed her housekeeper and wrote her letters. On the large desk that half filled this room there stood a missionary box with a slit in the top, and, although this slit had evidently been meant more for pennies than for half-crowns, Polly pushed the coin in and heard it drop with a clatter on to the other coins in the box.

Then she left the room and hurried away after Winnie.

As Polly followed Winnie upstairs she met Mrs. Grim on her way down and stood aside for her to pass. The housekeeper smiled at her approvingly.

"Good morning, Polly," she said. "I wish all my girls looked as fresh and neat as you do in the morning. Nobody would guess that you had been up a couple of hours or more. You look as blooming as a rose." She had a letter in her hand, the envelope possessing a deep black border, and after a moment's hesitation she held it out to Polly. "Take your apron off and run along to the Rectory with this, will you, my dear? Her ladyship gave it to Miss Edwards last night and told her to send Sam with it, but the idle young scamp was in bed and this morning he's

nowhere to be found. I've never seen such a boy for dis-
appearing when he's wanted! But it won't take you more
than a few minutes, and Winnie can start getting the trays
and bedroom cans ready for you by herself this morning,
when she has finished the dressing-room fireplace. It will
be good practice for her to use the brains the Almighty
gave her for once without depending on other people's,
and Doris will be up there along of Miss Edwards, so she
won't have time to idle before you get back." There was
very little, Polly thought, that escaped the housekeeper's
eye.

She ran downstairs again, slipping off her apron and
cap as she went, and went out of the back door into the
stable yard. The sunshine was warm on her face and the
fallen flowers of the pink chestnuts made a deep carpet
over the cobblestones there: the rooks had stopped their
scolding for a time, and the pigeons were cooing throatily
to one another in the dovecot under the stable roof, but
except for a horse that stamped with a metallic clatter in
its stall, and a cock that crowed triumphantly far away in
the village, other sign of life there was none. Polly drew a
deep breath and looked about her smilingly; she loved the
Manor best on a fine May morning.

She took the path that cut past the orchard and into the
park, open on one side to the parkland, and bounded on
the other, once the orchard wall was passed, by the tall
Rectory palings and the overhanging trees of its garden.
Four acres of garden went with the Rectory, and the
house had been enlarged by past generations of Harrobys
to accommodate Rectory children, who had usually far
outnumbered those at the Manor.

Polly hurried along, glad to be out in the lovely morning, but anxious to get back as soon as she could in case
Winnie incurred the wrath of Miss Edwards in her absence, that lady being rather touchy first thing in the
morning. She was not really looking where she was going
when the side gate in the Rectory fence ahead of her
opened suddenly and Charles Harroby stepped out on to
the path.

Charles had been at Windover for a month, and with

every day that passed he felt more relieved that the gift of the living there had now passed to the Squire's elder daughter, his cousin Ellen. If Sir John had been alive to command his gratitude and obedience it would have been impossible to refuse him, but as Ellen was more than willing to leave the selection of the new Rector to her mother, he felt free at last to choose his own future, and no longer bound to this small village, whose only importance lay in its proximity to the Manor.

This he made clear to Lady Augusta on the first evening of his arrival after old Lionel's death: he would come gladly, he told her, to take up the duties of the parish priest there as long as it was understood that he was only a locum-tenens until the new Rector came. He would be grateful, he added, if Ellen could find somebody else by the following autumn, as he had put his name forward for duties in the Colonies, and he felt himself to be more fitted for such a life.

Lady Augusta scolded and raged in vain, and finally, seeing that his mind was made up, she gave in. If he could reconcile such behavior with his conscience after all the Squire had done for him, she said, then she would say no more, but that did not prevent her from saying a great deal more for the space of two and a half hours, with a final intimation that she would never offer him any more help in his life, and that he need not expect it.

"I shall suggest that Ellen offers the living to poor Benjamin's eldest son Algernon," she said. Benjamin had been Sir John's youngest brother. "He wrote last week to ask if he could have it, but he is not a clever man, and his wife is a pushing little thing who never seems to know when she is not wanted. But at least poor Algy is a true Harroby, with great pride in his family. . . . Possibly my sister-in-law, your cousin Emily Harrison, might consent to come and keep house for you at the Rectory while you are there: she loves Windover and that bad-tempered old servant of hers has several relatives in the village. I know that Lionel's family intend to leave his furniture there until things are settled, and I don't suppose they will mind you using it."

So, in her high-handed way, did Lady Augusta continue to arrange other people's lives, and Charles was more thankful than ever that he had freed himself from her domination. Life under such conditions in Windover, for one of his temperament would have been insupportable. But at the same time he was willing to sign a truce with the lady, and he moved into the Rectory with Emily Harrison at the beginning of May.

Now in the old-fashioned books that Mrs. Grim lent Polly from time to time on a wet Sunday afternoon, quite a number of the characters were clergymen, and, if the reverend gentlemen did not turn out to be comsumptive and die lingering deaths in the last chapter, they would die so early in the story that their wives and families were reduced to terrible straits, quite unsuited to their station in life. Polly's idea about people's stations in life was as clearly defined as her ladyship's. But one thing was certain that die they must, and as inconveniently as possible, and in consequence these books that Mrs. Grim reserved for Sunday reading had given her a natural prejudice against clergymen. They appeared to her to be extremely thoughtless people, and most improvident where their families were concerned, and although young Mr. Charles looked as robust and handsome as ever, and as if consumption would never lay its dread finger upon him, and neither had he a wife and children to suffer if it did, yet the fact that he was a clergyman made Polly anxious to keep out of his way.

Polly had gone up in the world since that cold January evening when she had been driven out to Windover behind Charles and old Peters. Before the death of the Squire cut short entertaining at the Manor and plunged his widow into three years of mourning, grand relations of Lady Augusta's had come to stay from time to time, bringing with them their ladies' maids and valets. The round-eyed Polly, only a little older than Winnie was now, had listened to the wonderful stories those superior beings told of the houses where their employers had been entertained—some of them great mansions belonging to the first families in the land. According to the ladies' maids

such houses were like palaces, with State Rooms for entertaining Royalty, and every lady's maid had a footman behind her chair in the steward's room and the servants'
hall.

Polly heard about the silver breakfast-trays that were
taken upstairs, with hot-house peaches and champagne,
and little coffee-pots of solid gold. She heard of balls at-
tended by ladies with diamonds glittering in their hair,
and their dresses cut so low that you could see their shoul-
der-blades. It had formed in her young mind a magical,
princely world, where one day, if she took what opportunities came her way, she too might be lady's maid to some
great lady, and dine in the steward's room and have a
footman behind her chair. . . .

But in the meantime it was a morning in May and
Charles had not seen her and was striding off down the
path, and she ran after him, calling his name.

"Mr. Charles! Mr. Charles!"

He stopped then and looked back, and waited for her
to catch up with him, and smiled at her in the careless
way that he had smiled at the little drudge in the wagonette four years ago.

"Did you want me?" he asked.

"Yes, sir. It's a note, please, sir, from her ladyship."
She gave it to him breathlessly and waited for him to open
the black-bordered envelope. "I wasn't told if there was
an answer. Mrs. Grim did not say."

"The best way to find out then will be to open it, won't
it?" he said pleasantly, and he took a small pocket-knife
that hung from his watch-chain and slit the envelope while
she watched him, thinking how young he was to be a clergyman. The old Rector, the Reverend Lionel, had been
very old indeed: the village had put him down at ninety or
more, and he had had a way of smiling at you as if you
were not there, or as if his spirit was already in heaven
and sadly hampered by having its earthly body still clinging to it.

The note was short and written in Lady Augusta's
usual autocratic vein. It was not written in the third person, but Charles felt that it only just missed that form of

address: ever since he had refused the living he had been
conscious that she regarded him as a kind of inferior
beetle, permitted to crawl out from his skirting-board only
when told that he might.

My dear Charles, wrote her ladyship. *Certain things
have come to my notice that it is impossible for me to ig-
nore, and although I am ready to overlook them, being
aware of the temporary nature of your stay in Windover,
yet I would be obliged if you will make it convenient to
call upon me tomorrow morning at eleven o'clock, when I
will tell you my wishes in the matter. Please give my love
to Emily,*

> *Yours sincerely,*
> *A. Harroby*

The letter was dated the night before, and Charles's
chin set itself with more than a hint of defiance. She might
have a virtual say in the way he conducted the parish, as
Ellen appeared to have no interest in it, and she might order him to come and go at her bidding, but as it happened
he could not call at the Manor that morning because he
was burying old Mrs. Webb from the almshouses at that
hour. No doubt it was inconsiderate of the old lady's relatives not to have consulted Lady Augusta as to the time
when the curate-in-charge might be free to conduct the funeral service, but it could not be altered now.

Then, reminding himself that he was only there until
the autumn anyway, because Algy and his wife had accepted Ellen's offer of Windover with delight, he turned to
the maid who was waiting for his answer, and saw her
profile for the first time, and the knot of corn-colored hair
twisted up on the top of her head, and a chord of memory
struck somewhere in his mind.

"I've seen you before," he said. "Wait a moment, and it
will come to me! ... You are the little maid who drove
out with us one New Year's Day—it must be four years
ago now! ... Am I right?" He was so interested that Polly
found herself blushing.

"Please, sir, I'm Polly," she said hastily. "Polly Kettle."

"That's it! I remember because of the nursery rhyme, you know ... Little Polly Kettle, old Peters called you. He wouldn't call you that if he saw you now, though. You aren't little any longer, are you?"

"No, sir." But the blush had faded from Polly's face and she had returned to her old respectful self: she knew her place, did Polly, and she wasn't forgetting it, even for Mr. Charles's teasing. "I'm under-housemaid at the Manor now, sir."

"Are you indeed? That's promotion, I expect, isn't it?"

"Yes, sir." She remembered the bedroom cans and the early tea-trays and Winnie dropping things and spilling water on the carpets in the passages. "Please, sir, is there an answer?"

"What?" He was still staring at her in a disconcerting sort of way, but that was how the gentry went on sometimes, and you got used to it.

"An answer to the letter, sir," she repeated patiently, her eyes on the black-bordered envelope in his hand.

"Oh!" He seemed to recollect suddenly where he was, and his smile deepened. "No. There's no answer, thank you, Polly."

The church bell, giving its single call, told him that it was just on eight o'clock, and he walked on down the path to the churchyard, stuffing Lady Augusta's missive unceremoniously into his pocket, while Polly sped away to her bedroom cans and the early-morning trays.

The bell stopped as Charles arrived at the porch, and his old cousin Emily, who was the sole member of his congregation to attend his week-day services unless there happened to be clergy staying at the Manor, greeted him with a smile.

"What a lovely morning!" she said, lifting her face to kiss him. "Did you sleep well, dear?"

"Like a top, but then I always do." His eyes twinkled down at her. "That's the best of having a clear conscience!"

"I hope it's clear indeed," she said doubtfully. "But, whatever Augusta may say about it, I don't think my brother John is likely to haunt you, Charles!"

"Oh no. He was far too nice a person for that," said Charles lightly, and Emily Harrison looked at him with a touch of curiosity as he disappeared into the vestry. He had a strangely contrary nature, this nice young cousin of hers. In most ways so conscientious, it was strange that his broken promises to Sir John seemed to count for nothing at all. She wondered if there were other sides to his character that she had not yet discovered.

The service was soon over, because there was only the verger, old Herrick, to swell the ranks once he had stopped his bell-ringing, and as they walked back to the Rectory Charles showed her Lady Augusta's note.

"Oh, Charles!" she said, dismayed. "What have you been up to now? It looks as if you are on the carpet again!"

"Once more let me remind you that I have a clear conscience." He tucked his hand affectionately into her arm. "How nice it is to have you here to keep house for me, Cousin Emily! It is the only thought of Cousin Augusta's for which I can give her any credit. Tell me, what do *you* think I can have done or left undone that has merited such a peremptory summons?"

"It may be nothing to do with you," said Mrs. Harrison consolingly. "She has probably heard of some village misdemeanour that she is not able to tackle herself . . . something like theft, or drunkenness, you know, where a man's hand is a necessity. Dear Augusta dislikes drunkenness almost more than she does immorality."

"Do you think then that dear old Burke has come in roaring drunk at last, bless his wicked old heart? Or can one of the maids be in the family way?"

"Oh, my dear, Augusta would never send for you for *that!*" Mrs. Harrison was shocked. "You are much too young! Directly Mrs. Grim told her about it she would order the carriage and take the girl back to her mother herself."

"And scold her into a miscarriage, I suppose?" said Charles drily.

"Charles! You must control that tongue of yours, my

love! One of these days it is going to get you into serious trouble."

"I dare say it will, then." But he did not seem unduly concerned. They were passing the Rectory yard and from an open kitchen window there came the delicious aroma of frying bacon. "Umhm!" he said, lifting his head to sniff ecstatically. "I don't blame Algy for wanting this living, you know. . . . To come across the park and smell breakfast cooking on a lovely May morning . . . who would want the hair shirt of a slum living, when he might have all this?"

"I think," said Emily Harrison, "that dear Algy only has a little dry toast for his breakfast. He suffers from a bad digestion."

"Poor chap! What will he do with himself all day? Does he shoot or ride to hounds?"

"No. Poor Algy has never been robust enough to indulge in many country pursuits. . . . But as to what he will do with himself, I imagine he will do exactly as Augusta tells him, which will compensate her a little for having to endure Mrs. Algy on her doorstep as well. It's not that one dislikes the woman, you know, but she is rather tactless and tiresome."

"But perhaps she will be too much afraid of Cousin Augusta to be either," said Charles comfortingly. "And in the meantime I thank God I am not Algy, because I'm absolutely starving. . . ."

5

Up at the Manor Major Goodyer heard the distant summons of the church bell across the park, and turned over with a groan.

The worst of staying in country houses was that people got up at such unearthly hours. Take that church bell, for instance: he supposed that meant that Charles Harroby was taking a service down there at this moment, and on a week-day too, when most civilized people were still in bed. Nobody at the Manor appeared to have heard of having breakfast in bed, unless you were ill. You were expected to get up, and after attending morning prayers in the library, fill yourself up with enormous quantities of bacon-and-eggs and sausages and kippers and pigeon pie and kedgeree, making pleasant conversation in the meantime with Lady Augusta and her daughters and whatever guests had managed to find their way down to the dining-room too. And conversation at that hour of the morning did not suit the Major's disposition. He knew quite well that Crabb-Taylor would cut both prayers and breakfast, while Mrs. Crabb would twitter at him in an even more empty-headed fashion than usual.

The Crabb-Taylors were much addicted to country-house visiting, because the state of their finances made life in their small London house an extremely uncomfortable business: when their servants weren't sulking because they couldn't get their wages the tradesmen were dunning them for long-overdue bills.

The Major groaned again and opened a cautious eye to observe that his curtains had been drawn, and a tray of tea and bread-and-butter, cut wafer thin, placed beside his bed. Probably the maid had wakened him when she went out of the room: these servants crept about the place so quietly that you never knew they were there, and there wasn't one under forty, or worth looking at, except that pretty little housemaid Polly, and she fled from him as if he had the plague every time he tried to speak to her.

As his brain began its sluggish awakening with his body, he sat up and poured himself a cup of tea and went over in his mind the events of the day before.

Unexciting as his fortnight's stay at Windover had been, he felt that at last it was bearing fruit, and although from every angle that thought should have given him satisfaction, yet in point of fact it gave him no satisfaction at all.

It was all because of that girl—the pretty housemaid—whom he had happened to run into as she was coming down the corridor outside his room on the second morning of his stay. Her hands were full of brooms and brushes, her cheeks were flushed, and her eyes were full of youth and sparkle as she replied to something that was said to her by the giggling little country girl behind her.

And seeing her there in the wide corridor, with her yellow hair escaping from her cap, he had suddenly known to the full what it was that he had come to the Manor to do, and the whole venture lost its flavor and turned flat and stale. He knew that he was deliberately turning his back on gaiety, and pretty girls, and the life of a bachelor in London—which up to now had been a very pleasant one—and he was giving himself over to a boredom such as he had never known before; and just for a moment he had wavered, and thought seriously of sending himself an urgent summons back to London before it was too late.

And then he remembered the debts that had sent him to Crabb-Taylor for advice, and lighted a cigarette from the box that his man Giles had thoughtfully left beside his bed, though Lady Augusta had told him that she disliked the smell of tobacco in the bedrooms, and leaning back on the large pillows he smoked quickly and jerkily while he considered her daughter Ellen, who, if Crabb had spoken the truth, was a seventy-thousand pounder in her own right.

"Better come down to Windover with us in the summer

and meet Ellen," Crabb said at the club that night in the spring when the Major had declared himself to be cleaned out. "I dare say she'd have you. . . . She's never got on with her mother, and now the old man's gone I wouldn't be surprised if she doesn't look on matrimony with a more favorable eye."

But as it happened he did not have to wait until the summer to meet Ellen, because Crabb got him included in the Earl of Harrogate's house-party that Easter, when Ellen and Josey happened to be staying there with their uncle.

Of the two girls the Major preferred the younger: for all her ugly little monkeyish face, Josey had far more to say for herself, she was reputed to be a first-class shot, and she rode about the country on any mount that would take her, and, failing a horse, she was not averse to riding a bicycle instead. But unfortunately it was the cool, statuesque Ellen who was to have the money when she married, and Josey had nothing but her share after their mother went, and the Fanes, he learned from his stay with the Earl, who had inherited the title only after his father broke his neck in the hunting field, were a very long-lived family.

Ellen was no fool, however, and so from the start of their acquaintance he proclaimed himself to be a bit of an adventurer, a rolling stone, a man with the wanderlust in his blood, hoping that all this might shed a glamor about him that would appeal to a woman who had been subjected to thirty-two years of dependence and petty tryranny. The Major knew from experience that there were some women who were attracted to a rogue, half wishing to redeem him and the other half to mother him. And although he had no desire to be redeemed or mothered by Ellen, he did have a wish to pay the more pressing of his creditors before their number made his life as embarrassing and uncomfortable as the poor Crabb-Taylors'.

Until last night he had not known where he stood with Ellen. There were times when she smiled at him as if she believed every word he said, and thought him almost as fine a man as he thought himself, and there were others when he would catch a queerly thoughtful expression in her dark eyes as they rested upon him, as if their owner were weighing him up and doing it with care. Which was an improvement on Josey, who did not trouble to hide her dislike and contempt for him.

He had been asked for a fortnight's visit and today was the last day: Crabb and his wife were moving on to her family in Devon in the morning and he must put his fate to the test at once if he was to go back to London engaged to the elder Miss Harroby.

Last night he had been playing billiards with Crabb, comfortably aware that he was a much better player, and as they played, with Ellen and Josey and Mrs. Crabb looking on, the question of honesty cropped up, nobody quite knew how or why. Josey had started it, but he had discovered that Josey was like that: she would introduce unpleasant subjects into a perfectly innocent conversation and give it a nasty little twist that had never been intended.

With Crabb smiling lazily and taking no sides as he concentrated on the game, the Major had been provoked into declaring that everybody was dishonest at heart.

"If you see something that you want, your instinctive reaction is to get hold of it," he said. "That's not dishonesty, is it?" Across the green cloth, under the hanging shaded lamps, his eyes met Ellen's for a long moment, until she turned away and stared down into the fire. The billiard-room always had a fire burning in it in the evenings, summer and winter alike.

Josey caught the glance, however, and she laughed.

"It's the way you set about gaining the desirable object that can be honest or the reverse, surely?" she reminded him drily. She turned to Mrs. Crabb. "Do you remember that unpleasant old uncle of ours, Queenie, who used to leave half-crowns under the hearthrugs in his friends' country-houses, just to see if their servants were honest?"

"I can't say that I do, Josey." Queenie Crabb-Taylor was far more interested in her bracelets than the conversation. "Did he do it here?"

"Only once," said Josey with satisfaction. "I told the housemaids that when they found his half-crowns they were to paint them with treacle. . . . He didn't come and stay with us again after that."

"All the same," persisted the Major, "if I were to put half a crown under that hearthrug tonight, Miss Josey, I rather doubt if it would be there in the morning, and that is no reflection on the honesty of your servants. Half a crown is half a crown, after all. I would trust my man Giles with everything I've got, but I never leave money about because I don't consider that is playing fair." He also never had any money to leave lying about, but that was another story. "Don't you agree with me, Crabb?"

"Oh, absolutely. Our servants are nothing but a pack of thieves, but that is because I don't pay them." He bent over his cue while Ellen turned back from her contemplation of the fire to study the Major again, in her eyes the same thoughtfulness he had observed in them before, and for a few minutes the click of billiard-balls was the only sound in the room.

"I never know how much money I've got in my purse," said Queenie then plaintively. "So that if my maid helps herself to a half-sovereign now and then I'm none the wiser. But I don't see why I should shield her from temptation: it's supposed to develop one's character, isn't it?"

Nobody answered her. "If the Major wishes to leave his half-crown under the hearthrug," said Josey, "he has our full permission to do so. It will be there in the morning, because I would stake my life on the honesty of our servants, but I won't promise that it won't be covered in treacle!" She got up. "I'm going to bed, because I shall be up early tomorrow, pigeon-shooting. Burke says they're becoming a pest, and if either of you two gentlemen feel like joining us I'm sure he will welcome you. But you'll have to be in the lower spinney just after five."

"Not for me, thanks," said Crabb, laughing, and the Major said that he too enjoyed his sleep, and then Queenie asked her husband if he did not think they ought to spend a little while with Aunt Augusta, as it was their last evening.

"Most certainly I do, my dear," said Crabb. "This fellow is too good for me, anyway, and I've lost enough money to him for one evening." And he followed her in the direction of the small drawing-room, leaving Ellen alone with the Major.

Archie Goodyer took a half-crown from his pocket and tossed it smilingly in his hand.

"Shall I take Josey at her word and hide it?" he asked Ellen. "Are your servants to be sheltered and shielded ... as you have been all your life, Miss Ellen?"

"I don't understand you." Yet in spite of her coolness she hurried a little over the words. "In what way have I been sheltered and shielded, Major Goodyer?"

"Have you not, then? What did your father allow you to see or know of the world beyond Windover? Oh, I dare say once a year you went to London for the season—"

She stopped him with a laugh.

"It's many years now since we did that. When Josey and I were girls, naturally we were taken to London by our parents, and after having made our curtsys at a drawing-room we were thrown into the marriage market with the rest of our generation. But by the time Josey's third season—and my fifth—came round, the Pater thought any further effort in that direction would be wasted, and he was perfectly right. I found nobody among the vapid young men there who could even faintly interest me, while Josey was always happier in the saddle than in the ballroom. And besides, although pretty girls—even if they are penniless—may sometimes find husbands at a London ball, plain ones can very seldom bring it off so successfully."

"But you are not penniless now?" The words slipped out in an unguarded moment, and her dark eyes came round to his face and saw the color mount there with a gleam of satisfaction.

"At the moment I am as penniless as ever I was," she reminded him quietly. "Years ago an old great-aunt left me all her fortune, to be paid over to me only on my wedding-day. She made the bequest at a time when I was very unhappy, and she did it out of the kindness of her heart, never dreaming that by the time she died such a legacy would only end in making me the laughing-stock of the neighborhood."

For the first time there was a trace of emotion in her calm voice, and, in spite of his selfishness, pity for her stirred in him.

"Not a laughing-stock!" he protested quickly. "Never! You have far too much dignity for that."

She shrugged her shoulders.

"Oh," she said, "I have got over it by this time, even if some of our friends have not. I don't need any man's compassion, Major Goodyer!"

"I am sure you do not. Pity for you would be an insult, Miss Ellen. Your spirit is too fine . . . and far too independent."

She caught eagerly at the last word.

"Independent," she repeated. "Yes, that is a word that I like . . . but I can only win independence in one way, by marriage, and the man who marries me, though he may have seventy thousand excellent reasons for doing so, will have to mind what he is about, because I happen to price myself rather high."

She put up her head and stood so for a moment by the fire, her tall figure in its dowdy black evening gown erect and defiant, her foot in its beaded slipper tapping the fender impatiently. He came to her quickly and stood beside her, but he made no attempt to touch her.

"You could not set such a high price on yourself as the one I would set, Ellen," he said humbly. "If you want your independence so badly I would be proud and happy to be allowed to give it to you."

The cold face softened and for a moment her eyes glowed with real feeling.

"Archie," she said in a low voice, "I think you are a rogue . . . but a likable one."

He dared to take her hand.

"Then you will marry me?" he asked, hoarse with excitement. Seventy thousand pounds, he thought . . . seventy thousand pounds . . . it was too good to be true.

She took her hand away.

"I don't know," she said coolly. "I will think about it."

"But I go back to London tomorrow!" he said urgently. "I can't go without knowing ... without having your promise. ..."

She hesitated, and seeing her uncertainty and suddenly afraid lest he should lose the glittering prize after all, he held up the half-crown and placed it under the rug at their feet with a flourish.

"There!" he said. "Meet me tomorrow morning here in this room, at nine o'clock before prayers. We'll see if your sister's boast is correct ... and you shall give me your answer then!"

He saw her smile.

"Very well," she said finally. "Tomorrow at nine, in this room." She said good night quickly and escaped any further demonstrations he might feel impelled to give, but she need not have been afraid: her suitor felt that he had done quite enough.

And now the morrow had come, and if he meant to be in the billiard-room by nine he would have to get up.

He finished his tea slowly, looked at the thin bread-and-butter with distaste, and dropped his cigarette stub into the cup as Giles came in with his shaving water, followed by Albert with the tin tub for his bath.

Giles directed the young footman where he was to put it, and watched him as he brought in a large can of cold water, and after he had gone he began to put out his master's clothes.

"You may put out the Norfolk suit, Giles," said the Major, watching him. "We shall not be returning to London until this afternoon ... and we might even be staying on for another day or so."

"Indeed sir?" The man permitted himself his usual thin smile. "Well, it's a pleasant time of year for the country, May is, though I prefer town myself."

The Major yawned. "You wouldn't like to live in the country all the year round, then?" he said.

Giles shot him a calculating glance. "It would depend on the circumstances, wouldn't it, sir?"

The Major frowned. "I'm thinking of getting married," he said shortly.

"Yes, sir." Giles did not seem surprised, although in his aggravating way he pretended not to understand. "Is it Miss Josey, sir?"

"No it isn't, confound you. It's Miss Ellen."

"Indeed, sir?" Was there disapproval in Giles's thin back, or was he just being more irritating than usual? The trouble was that he knew too much. "They say in the servants' hall here, sir, that she's a deep one, is Miss Ellen," he remarked calmly.

"Oh? Who says so?"

"Well, sir, it's just servants' gossip, as you might say. They say that Miss Josey is always open and above-board, and you know where you are with her. If she doesn't like you, or the way you do anything, she will tell you so and make no bones about it. . . . But Miss Ellen is different, and you never know what she is thinking . . . but I'm sure she's a very nice lady."

"That's enough, Giles."

"Yes, sir." The man poured the water into the bath, placed the towels on a chair beside it, and went away, and the Major got up. Never, since he had resigned his commission, had he felt so uncertain about his future.

"Confound the fellow!" he said as he stripped off his nightshirt and stepped into the bath. "Servants' gossip . . . that's just about all it is. What do they know about it?"

But as he scrubbed with soap and sponge he scowled, remembering Ellen's cool smile, and her remark that she priced herself high. Would it be too great a price? he wondered uneasily. Surely not . . . surely he would be able to get round her as he'd got round others as aloof and cool.

He dressed carefully and went downstairs to the billiard-room as the clocks were striking nine. The windows of the room were of stained glass, in order to shut out a view of the stable yard, which in day-time gave it a gloomy appearance, not helped by the fact that it faced north.

Miss Harroby did not keep him waiting long: at five minutes past the hour she entered the room dressed in gray trimmed with black. The colors did not suit her and neither did the style: Ellen was too tall and angular for the hour-glass fashion of the day.

But the Major did not look at her dress: it was her face that he examined most anxiously, and it was as composed as ever.

"So here you are!" he said, advancing towards her with an eagerness that might have been attributed to the impatience of a lover. "I thought you had forgotten. . . ."

"Good morning, Major Goodyer." She held out her hand to him with a smile. "No, I had not forgotten our appointment."

He wished she would not make it sound like a business arrangement. He wondered if he should say that she had given him a sleepless night, and decided against it, knowing that she would not believe him. He said in a voice that he tried to make as cool as hers:

"And have you decided what to do?"

"I have." She withdrew her hand. "I have made up my mind to take advantage of your offer, Archie."

"You mean . . . you will marry me?" Seventy thousand pounds. . . . He forgot his misgivings and his spirits soared. "Ellen, is this true? You aren't having me on?"

"It is quite true." Her smile was a trifle warmer now. "We are not yet out of mourning for my father, but I think the wedding could take place at the end of June without giving an impression of indecent haste."

"The end of June?" He drew a deep breath, his mind dwelling on the almost unlimited credit that would now be his with this sudden opening of the door to wealth. "If it cannot be any sooner, then the end of June must do." He took her hand again in both of his and held it against his chest. "And Ellen . . . I will never betray your trust in me. That I do most solemnly swear, on my honor as a gentleman!"

Her smile deepened, but her eyes were as impersonal as ever, and for a second time that morning uneasiness touched him, as he remembered Giles and the gossip about her. It was hard indeed to read Ellen's thoughts. He stooped quickly to kiss her, but she moved as swiftly, so that his lips only brushed her cheek, and then she disengaged her hand.

"And now," she said briskly, "having settled that, before we join the others in the library for prayers, let us see if your half-crown is still under that rug!"

But of course his half-crown had gone.

6

OLD Billings, the postman, was late that morning, because he had stopped on the way at the almshouse to ask what time the funeral was to be. Mrs. Webb was his wife's cousin and Mrs. Billings had told him that he was to go to the funeral with her.

The pull up to the Manor seemed a long one and he was relieved when a voice behind him offered to relieve him of the letters for the house.

"James! Now that's very kind of you, lad, to save an old man's legs." He slung the bag off his shoulder and gave the Manor's bundle of letters into James's hands, thinking as he did so what a fine fellow young Burke had grown into. Tall and broad-shouldered, with those gray-blue eyes and crisply curling hair, he was as handsome as they came. "Saw you coming up the lane with that pretty little Polly Kettle again last Sunday evening," he said. "Are you courting, then, James? Because you didn't seem to be making the most of your opportunities to my way of thinking!"

James flushed.

"Me and Polly's just good friends," he said shortly. "She's always thought of me as she would of a brother, if she had one."

"H'm." The old man's eyes were sly. "Well, I should have said she was a sight too pretty to inspire a deal of brotherly love in a young man like you, James, but maybe I'm wrong. I'll bet that Albert up at the Manor don't think of her as a sister, neither!"

"Polly wouldn't look at Albert," said James scornfully, and then stopped, because although Polly might confide her secret dreams to him, they were not to be tossed about all over the village. "I'll take these letters up to the house right away, Mr. Billings."

"Aye, do. And mind you give 'em into Mr. Harris's own hands too. He allus likes to have fust look at all the letters what comes to the Manor, does Mr. Harris."

"I'll give them to him," said James, and he went off up the avenue, frowning because the old man's teasing had started a train of thought in his mind.

He knew that Albert, as well as most of the other young men who worked on the estate, had asked Polly to walk out with him, and she had laughed at him and at the others, because she had told him so as they walked back together on Sunday evenings from the gamekeeper's cottage.

She wasn't going to tie herself down at eighteen, she said with a toss of her golden head. What could a footman offer her, or a cowman, or a farm laborer, come to that? She wasn't going to be like her Aunt Ada, burdened with children and taking in washing to put bread into their mouths. And neither would she marry a groom or a gardener. You might get a cottage thrown in, and perks and that, but it was a hard and unrewarding sort of life unless you were in love with your man.

"And there isn't one of the men that work on the estate, James," she told him solemnly, "that I could ever fall in love with."

"Except me," he said, teasing her, and she had laughed and slipped her hand into his arm and given it a little shake.

"Oh *you!*" she said. "But you don't count . . . you are just James, the most dependable, wonderful person I've ever known!"

Her praise made his heart swell with gratitude, because although he had loved her from the moment he saw her on that January afternoon four and a half years ago, he would not have dreamed of telling her so. He knew that she was not ready yet for loving, his little Polly. She had to grow up a bit, and she had to learn a whole lot more about life and people and the way she wished to tread. Her head was still filled with romantic dreams of great houses, and the grand, titled folk who lived in them, and the ladies' maids who had footmen behind their chairs. Love to Polly was a thing of the future, mixed up with silver breakfast-trays and hot-house peaches and champagne.

Had she not told him that she was just biding her time until the opportunity came her way—as come it must—for her to go on and up, into the service of the great?

"Who knows, James," she said breathlessly, her eyes like stars. "I might end up as Lady's maid to a Royal Princess . . . Why, it might be to Princess May herself. . . ."

The glitter and the gold and the dreaming . . . It would not harm her, though, any more than it harmed a child to read a fairy tale.

And with his frown fading at the thought of her he strode on up the avenue to put the bundle into Harris's hands, never thinking that among those letters was one that would alter the course of Polly's life, and tear her dreams ruthlessly apart.

Mrs. Grim always came to the little morning-room at ten o'clock to discuss with Lady Augusta the orders for the day. Accounts were gone through once a month, because her ladyship prided herself on the excellence with which she kept track of every penny she spent, and arrangements were made in advance for the entertainment of the Manor's guests.

Today, nearly eighteen months since she was widowed, Lady Augusta was seriously considering starting her At Home days again, which had always been the first Thursday in every month. In discussing this with her housekeeper, sitting erect and dignified in her widow's weeds, Lady Augusta remarked that she felt she had no right to spoil the enjoyments of others with her own private grief any longer.

"I have my daughters to consider after all, Mrs. Grim," she said.

"Yes, m'lady."

"And then there is another thing," went on Lady Augusta, taking up a letter from the small pile of correspondence at her elbow. "I have had a letter this morning from Mrs. Julius Fane. She tells me that Captain Fane's regiment has been ordered to India at the end of next month, and much as she would have liked to accompany him, unfortunately their little boy is still far from strong. You remember, Mrs. Grim, how they nearly lost him with pneumonia last Christmas, and Mrs. Julius feels that to expose him to the heat and unhealthy conditions in India just now might be extremely dangerous. She has asked me if I will take him and his two sisters here at Windover for the summer. She will join them directly the Captain sails, and I see no reason why I should not have them; in fact, it will be very pleasant to have the old nurseries opened up again, and children about the place will interfere with nobody. Their own nurse and nursery-maid will come with them and I don't think it should give a great deal of extra trouble to the servants."

"No, m'lady." Mrs. Grim considered the problem, her black beady eyes darting this way and that. Captain the Hon. Julius Fane was the third son of the Earl of Harrogate, and a great favorite with his aunt at the Manor, and very popular with her servants. "There's the extra cooking of course for the nursery meals, but Cook won't mind that. She never makes a trouble of anything, doesn't Cook. And there will be the hot water to take up for the baths, but Winnie can help the nursery-maid there, and with the trays, too. . . . And then there's the fires, but the boy will take the coals up. He is a good strong lad, this boy we have now, and very willing."

"Very well. That is settled, then. I will write today to Mrs. Julius and tell her that we shall be delighted to see her family next week. Can the beds be aired and the rooms ready in time?"

"Oh yes, my lady." Mrs. Grim waited, guessing from her ladyship's manner that she had something more to say.

Certainly Lady Augusta had something to say, and she did not like saying it. She looked perturbed and anxious, and, at the same time, if such a thing were possible, a trifle guilty as well.

"There is one more thing before you go, Mrs. Grim," she said. "Something rather disturbing happened here last night ... or perhaps I should say this morning. I must question you about this, and I do beg you not to misunderstand me when I ask you if you are sure of the ... honesty ... of all our maids here?"

The housekeeper was for a moment too taken aback to reply, and then her surprise changed to indignation and Lady Augusta saw it and did not blame her for it in the least. Mrs. Grim had been housekeeper at the Manor for a long time and they knew and respected each other.

"I took up every reference, my lady," said Mrs. Grim when she could trust herself to speak, her face flushed deep red and her black eyes snapping. "I always have done ever since I've been here as housekeeper. I would not dream of engaging a girl unless I knew that she had a good character and came from honest, hard-working parents. And I don't think I've often been mistaken, either. There's some like that Winnie that is rough, naturally, when they first come, but Winnie is only fourteen, as most of them are when they start, and they tone down wonderfully in time and make very good maids, as she will. Winnie has the makings of a very excellent maid in her, though not perhaps in what you might call the superior class of servant—"

"I know, Mrs. Grim. I am sure of it." Lady Augusta attempted to stem the flow of the housekeeper's indignation. "It is most annoying for me to be compelled to make such an enquiry, every bit as annoying as it is for you to have to listen to it. But it all comes through a joke—a very stupid joke—on the part of one of my guests. Major Goodyer left a half-crown under the hearthrug in the billiard-room last night." She caught the gleam in the housekeeper's eye and hurried on. "I know exactly what you are feeling, because I felt the same myself directly I heard about it. It was a stupid and, in fact, an unkind prank to play. But the fact remains, Mrs. Grim, that this morning the half-crown was not there."

Mrs. Grim's outraged expression said "Serve him right!" But all she said aloud was a prim: "I will make enquiries, my lady. Will that be all?" and she took her departure in an unsmiling silence that showed to the full the height and depth of her anger against the Major.

In due course Polly was called to the housekeeper's room and questioned sternly as to the whereabouts of the missing half-crown, and she flushed and laughed and bit her lip and finally confessed.

"Yes, Mrs. Grim, I saw the half-crown there," she said calmly. "Left under the rug where Winnie and me would find it. I told Winnie not to touch it, but after she had gone I thought to myself, 'It's unlucky to find silver and let it lie!' My Auntie Ada often told me so. 'You must give it away directly you find it,' she said, 'or it won't bring you any luck at all.' So I looked round to see where I could give it, and the only thing I could think of was her ladyship's box for the poor people of Africa that stands on her desk in the little morning-room, and so I went and dropped it in there. I hope I didn't do wrong, ma'am? If her ladyship likes to open her box she will find the half-crown there, I give you my word."

Polly's eyes were guileless and innocent, and Mrs. Grim was startled and full of admiration, although she would not have dreamt of saying so because it would not have done. She told Polly waspishly that she needn't think she had done anything clever, because she hadn't, and didn't she know she might have cast suspicion on poor little Winnie, being as she was the youngest and newest maid at the Manor? She couldn't think what Polly had been thinking of to do such a stupid thing, and she was never to do it again. But there was a twinkle in her eyes and a twist at the corner of her mouth, and as she went to the door she gave her a pat on the arm and said:

"I shall have to tell her ladyship what has happened, of course, but without mentioning any names."

Polly went back to her sweeping and dusting with a light heart, while the housekeeper stalked back with dignity to Lady Augusta.

Major Goodyer and Ellen, and the Crabb-Taylors and Josey, had joined her ladyship in the library after breakfast and Mrs. Grim did not look at any of them as she marched up to her employer and said, meeting her straight in the eye:

"I have spoken to the maids who did the hearth in the billiard-room this morning, my lady, and one of them admitted that she saw the half-crown under the rug there and picked it up. But she is a superstitious girl, and she thought it would be unlucky to keep money that she found unexpectedly like that, and so she gave it away to that box on your table in the morning-room."

Lady Augusta's gasp was echoed by Ellen and Mrs. Crabb. Josey's eyes were turned rather maliciously to the Major, and Crabb himself gave a guffaw of laughter. Then Lady Augusta said with a return to her usual dignity: "Thank you, Mrs. Grim. That will be all."

"Thank *you*, my lady!" Mrs. Grim went out of the room triumphantly, and as the door closed behind her Ellen said in her decided way, "I wish I knew when Grimmie is being impertinent, but I never do, and I don't suppose I ever shall!"

"Grimmie is *never* impertinent!" cried Josey indignantly, while Crabb said unkindly:

"Archie has certainly lost his half-crown at all events. Your maids, Josey, appear to be not only honest but generous as well!"

"*If* the half-crown is in the box, of course," retorted the Major disagreeably. "I don't think that was a very likely story, you know! But the poor girl had to think of something when your dragon of a housekeeper tackled her with it, and I must say I admire her for it. It shows a quick brain and a lively imagination."

Lady Augusta raised the lorgnettes that hung from her waist on a gold chain and looked at him through them unsmilingly.

"Would you know your half-crown if you saw it, Major Goodyer?" she asked coldly.

"Would I?" Rather at a disadvantage because of the lorgnettes, he considered the lost coin for a moment in silence. "Well, except that it was a Jubilee one—1887, you know—I can't recall that it was very different from any other."

"Thank you. Then perhaps you will do me the service of coming to the morning-room with me, and we will examine the contents of that box together." His hostess, as awe-inspiring as a schoolmistress, rose to her feet and led the way to the morning-room, and he was forced to accompany her, while the others followed.

Her ladyship went at once to the writing-table and opened a drawer in it and took from it a small, mother-of-pearl-handled knife. With this she slit the label that covered the bottom of the box, and through the hole thus revealed there cascaded out a shower of coins on to the blotting-pad. Pennies, half-pennies, tiny silver threepenny pieces, a sixpence or two, and even two half-sovereigns; all were there in some considerable number. But there was only one half-crown.

Lady Augusta picked it up and examined it and saw the year 1887 on it, and handed it to the Major.

"That," she said forbiddingly, "is yours, I take it?"

"Lady Augusta, I couldn't . . . really I wouldn't—" He broke off, red with embarrassment, while Josey gave a small snort of laughter.

"You will take back your half-crown, if you please, Major Goodyer," said Lady Augusta with her usual determination. "And I should be grateful if you will refrain from such stupid jokes if you ever come to my house again. It is not the kind of thing that amuses me, however much it may amuse my daughters." Here her eyes rested coldly on her younger daughter, but unexpectedly it was Ellen who met the challenge with a firmness equal to her mother's.

"You are taking this far too seriously, Mater," she said calmly. "It *was* only a joke, after all."

"There are some things, Ellen, that I insist on taking seriously, as you well know. And doubt cast on the integrity of my servants is one of them." Lady Augusta took a fresh label from her drawer and pasted it over the hole in the box and sealed it. Then she put the money back in the box, foraged in the pocket of her underskirt for her purse, and took from it a half-crown to replace the one that she had just returned to the Major.

But he could not let it rest there without losing countenance for ever with his future mother-in-law. He thrust his hand into his pocket and from the handful of coins that he brought from it he selected a gold sovereign.

"Allow me then to pay a forfeit for my stupidity," he said, and with an air of somewhat forced gallantry he slipped it through the slit in the box after Lady Augusta's half-crown.

"Well, that's very generous of you, Major Goodyer," she said, slightly mollified, but even so she was quite unprepared for her eldest daughter's next remark, as she came up to the Major's side and thrust her hand into his arm.

"As for Archie coming to the Manor again, Mater," Ellen said, smiling at her mother with the light of battle in her eyes, "I'm afraid he will be here quite often from now on—or at least until the end of June, when he and I are going to be married."

"*Married?* . . . Ellen, have you taken leave of your senses?" Lady Augusta was too taken aback to choose her words, while Josey stood staring helplessly from her sister to the Major and back again, and the Crabb-Taylors said nothing at all. Major Goodyer drew Ellen's hand more closely into his arm and stroked it tenderly, and while she did not appear to respond to this caress, neither did she remove her hand. Her whole attention was fixed on the battle ahead of her.

"I have not taken leave of my senses," she told her mother quietly. "And neither am I too young this time to know my own mind."

"I should think not, indeed!" Lady Augusta found her voice with an effort. "You are over thirty, Ellen, far too old to allow yourself to be duped by this . . . adventurer."

"It is always a mistake to descend to abuse, Mater, as you have often said yourself," Ellen reminded her coolly. "Nothing is gained by it and in fact the whole conversation is merely vulgarized, which I am sure you never intended." She took her hand from her betrothed. "I think the rest should leave us now until we have finished what there is to be said between us."

They took the hint, and as it was nearly time for the carriage to come round to take the Crabb-Taylors to the station, they stayed only to congratulate Archie before going away upstairs to get ready for their journey.

The Major found himself outside the closed morning-room door with Josey.

"I can't leave your sister to face the music alone," he said, looking back uncertainly over his shoulder, but Josey only laughed.

"Don't be afraid," she said lightly. "You won't lose Ellen. She is determined to have you—I saw it from the moment we met you at my uncle's at Easter. And when she started talking about her independence on the way home I knew that the day was lost."

"Don't you believe in independence for women then, Miss Josey?"

"It depends on the cost, Major Goodyer."

"Does that mean that to have me as a husband would be too high a cost for you to pay?"

She shook her head and sighed.

"If you are to be my brother-in-law you must learn not to ask me leading questions!" she said. "I have a disconcerting habit of blurting out the truth. Let us go and admire the first roses of the summer until Ellen is ready for you."

What Ellen had to say to her mother was never known, because neither she nor her mother spoke of it again. But when she came to find her future husband Miss Harroby's head was held high and there was a look of triumph in her eyes.

"It is all settled," she told Josey briefly. "Archie and I are to be married at the end of July, not June, as the Mater doesn't think she will be able to get the invitations out in time."

Josey murmured her lukewarm congratulations, and left it to Ellen's fiancé to applaud her for the way she had handled things.

"Then all I have to do now is to find somewhere for us to live, my dear," he added.

"Oh yes, that goes without saying." Ellen dismissed the

matter carelessly. "I have decided to have a house in London for the present. The Mater and I will be going to London next week to see the dressmakers, and also my lawyers, and I will look for a house to rent there for a time."

He tried to be gallant still, although in the face of this high-handed management of their affairs such gallantry was almost reduced to rags.

"But I shall go to London this afternoon as I had arranged, all the same," he said with a rather dreadful archness. "There is the matter of a ring to be chosen."

Josey wondered how her sister could endure him. Given his head, the man's conceit would lead to a bumptious assurance that would make most men long to kick him. After the carriage that had taken the Crabb-Taylors to the station in the morning bore him away from them in the afternoon, she could stand it no longer.

"So it is done!" she cried reproachfully when she was alone with Ellen. "You have traded your money for your peace of mind. I don't know how you could endure to do it!"

"On the contrary, I have traded nothing," said Ellen coolly. "I cannot touch my fortune unless I have a husband, and Archie Goodyer is head over heels in debt and needs a rich wife to satisfy his creditors. Very well. The bargain has been made, although the terms of it may be discussed very much later—after the wedding ceremony."

Josey stared at her sister.

"Are you really so heartless and cold-blooded?" she wondered. "Or are you trying to hit back at this man because another treated you badly in the past? Because if that is it, Ellen and if you are trying to hurt this worthless creature, Archie Goodyer, simply because Roger Blackstone hurt you years ago, you are only descending to his level. And for that I would never have given you credit, however badly you want your independence."

"But that, my dear, is because independence means nothing to you and everything to me. I have no romantic dreams of love and happiness. Those were torn to pieces years ago by my father and Roger Blackstone between

them, and it seems to me now that I have obeyed other people and put my own wishes on one side long enough. The future—my future—is going to be my affair."

"I wonder if you are right?" Josey was distressed for her. "Ellen, if I can see through this man surely you can. . . . You've always been much wiser than me, and I've admired and looked up to you all my life. I'd hate to see you humiliated and hurt."

"What is all this talk about being hurt?" said Ellen, laughing. "What a sentimental little creature you are, Josey, under your queer, gruff ways! I lost all power of being hurt when my father turned Roger out of the house and he went, without a protest. . . . My heart, if I ever had one, died then, and I only waited for Roger's marriage to give it a decent burial. Now let's talk no more about it. Let's talk instead about the house I intend to rent in town. . . . There was one advertised in Portman Square in *The Times* this morning. I like Portman Square. It is a most convenient district."

Josey tried once more. "And will you choose to live in London, with a husband like Major Goodyer to spend your money?"

"Archie will only spend what I allow him to spend," Ellen said quietly. "That is one of the terms of the bargain that I intend to discuss with him after the ceremony has set me free."

And hearing the tone of her sister's voice, and seeing the expression in her dark eyes, for the first time since she had known him Josey felt sorry for the Major.

7

IT was scarcely surprising that Lady Augusta did not feel
equal to seeing Charles when he arrived in answer to her
note that afternoon, and was in two minds about sending
him away again. But when he apologized for not having
come in the morning, as she had wished, she was still so
shattered as to be unusually gracious.

"Of course you could not come," she said. "It was Old
Biddy Webb's funeral, wasn't it? I was told about it—in
fact I believe the Manor sent a wreath. She was Cook
here years ago, you see, and we like to remember our old
servants. I recall how angry your cousin John was when
her son refused to be our groom and insisted on going off
into the Army instead. Poor Biddy. She was in tears about
it, and I must say we all thought he was too good a man
to mix himself up with all that riff-raff, but he would go.
He said he wanted to see the world, if you please! Well,
he saw India, poor fellow, and died of cholera there. He'd
have done much better if he had been our groom."

Charles refrained from commenting on young Webb's
stupidity, and after a sharp glance at him Lady Augusta
went on in a tone she intended to be severe, but because
of what she had undergone that morning succeeded only
in being slightly querulous:

"I wanted to see you on rather a serious matter,
Charles. At least, it may not appear serious to you, but in
a village like Windover you cannot be too careful. I understand that after the cricket match on Saturday—the
first of the season—you supplied both elevens with beer!"

Charles suppressed a smile with difficulty.

"Why yes, Cousin Augusta, I did," he admitted cheerfully. "It was a very warm afternoon, and our eleven had

done very well and played a corking good game, and they were all very thirsty. I know that Cousin John always used to supply beer for their teas."

"But since your cousin died I have not done so, Charles, because I consider that tea and lemonade quench their thirst just as effectively. They are perfectly aware of my feelings in this matter, and I am not aware that anyone has complained."

"They would not dare! And it was my doing alone. Tea and lemonade were sent down with the food from the Manor here, but I remembered Cousin John saying once that a village cricket match was not a Manor tea-party, and nor was it a schoolchildren's treat! And so, as it was very warm, I supplied the beer."

She was too upset to reply. She felt old and very much alone this afternoon, she missed the gossipy hours she used to spend with old Lionel, and she was angry at Charles's reference to his cousin John. The Squire had been too much inclined to encourage the drinking of beer among the villagers, in her opinion. Why, there was the barrel that always stood inside the back door, so that any casual tramp could help himself to it if he felt inclined that way. She had soon put a stop to that, and Lionel had backed her up. Lionel saw at once that it would not do, just as he would have seen that this engagement of Ellen's would not do. He would have come to the rescue this morning with some suggestion that would have put sense into Ellen and routed the detestable Archie Goodyer right away.

Charles had never been a favorite of hers, and since he had behaved with such base ingratitude for all that Sir John had done for him she had no patience with him. He looked younger than ever since he had shaved off his long fair moustache, and she did not feel that she could depend on him at all. She could only grumble at him indirectly for being unable to advise or help her.

"And there's another thing I wanted to talk to you about, Charles," she said. "I know you haven't been ordained very long, and that good sermons come with experience—dear old Lionel was so excellent—but *was* it necessary to go into all those sordid details about the conditions in your friend's slum parish as you did last Sunday? We all know that such things exist, and that in the poorer quarters of our big cities poverty can be a terrible thing, and I am sure Mr. Latimer is doing his best, although I always distrust people who rant about the conditions of the working classes! But I can see no reason at all why we should have our feelings harrowed by it all down here in Windover! It is nothing to do with us!"

"Is it not?" he said. His young face looked rather thoughtful. "But don't you think that smugness and complacency can be as terrible in their way as the very real physical poverty of a London slum? There can be a poverty of the spirit. . . ."

"Thank you, Charles, you are not in the pulpit now! And I am sorry that we strike you as being complacent and . . . what was the other word you used?"

"Smug," he put in calmly. "Well, I'm sorry too, Cousin Augusta, but I do think some of your friends are smug. They will subscribe to all sorts of good causes abroad, and think nothing of what goes on here at home. Why, I've seen men of forty blinded for life and out of work for the rest of their days, through accidents in steel foundries and chemical works. I have seen young girls of fourteen apprenticed to forging iron chains, and women making slippers from seven in the morning to eight at night, and do you know what pay they get for all this? The chemical and foundry worker is lucky if he gets thirteen shillings a week, and if he happens to be blinded he can pray to die quickly, because there is no compensation for him and no money for him to live on; the girls at the forges make on an average four shillings a week, the women in the shoe factories as little as two—or sometimes even three ha'pence a day—all being paid, you see, on piecework. That's sweated labor in our big, industrial country; that's our wonderful, prosperous empire on which the sun never sets. . . ."

Lady Augusta moved restlessly and wished more than ever that she had the Squire with her, or the old Rector to set this young man down firmly in his place. Dear old

Lionel could be very crushing when he liked, and that was what Charles needed—crushing.

"Charles," she said, getting up to show him that the interview was at an end, "you are talking like one of these dreadful, ranting Socialists! Please let me hear no more of it. This kind of talk may go down well at Oxford, in the rooms of undergraduates with adolescent minds, but it does not *do* down here with *us* and I will not *have* it! I don't want to ask the Bishop to find me somebody else until Algy is free to come here in September, but if you persist in this ... ridiculous nonsense ... I shall not hesitate to do so."

He sighed.

"Would you like to see copies of my sermons before I get up into the pulpit on Sundays, Cousin Augusta?" he asked meekly, and saw her flush.

"I hope that will not be necessary," she said, but on the following Sunday she was sorry that she had not agreed to the suggestion, because the little church was packed, and the young man who had drawn the crowd there electrified his congregation by leaning down from the pulpit and demanding: "Your money or your life! Which are you going to give in charity to your neighbor?"—his face more like a schoolboy's than ever above his white surplice.

Lady Augusta was so angry that she could scarcely sit still under what she called the tirade of rubbish that followed, and when she left the church she could hardly bring herself to speak civilly to Emily Harrison, who, she considered, encouraged Charles in his radical notions.

"I think Charles has some very strange friends, Emily," she said stiffly as she walked to the lychgate beside her sister-in-law. "Most of them appear to be dock-hands and factory workers, from what I can make out. And what is more they appear to be giving him some most peculiar ideas."

Mrs. Harrison's blue eyes regarded her thoughtfully.

"He has a curious personality," she agreed. "You can never run across Charles without striking a few sparks, although in the main he is a dear, good-natured fellow, and in spite of his fiery ideas, inclined to be curiously indolent.

But he never wished to go into the Church, you know, Augusta, and I think it was a pity that John insisted on it. But there you are—it is done now, and he will have to make the best of it. His mother thinks he'll be a bishop one day if he goes on as he is doing now, and I'd never be surprised if he were. He likes getting things done, as long as he can do them in his own way, and he doesn't give a fig for anybody's opinions."

"I have noticed that," said Lady Augusta ominously. "I understand that the cricket elevens were again given beer with their tea last night, Emily, in spite of my strict orders to the contrary!"

"Oh no, dear! Only tea and lemonade with their *tea!*" Emily's eyes were innocent, and as round as buttons. "Charles gave it out before the match started. . . . He said that you were most kindly providing tea for the two elevens in the church hall after the match, as usual, with tea and lemonade. And then he said that after they had finished, if any of them cared to step round to the Harroby Arms they would be treated to a pint of beer by the curate-in-charge of the parish and that the winning teams would get two pints apiece!" She chuckled softly. "Lord Windover was talking to me about it before this morning's service. He said he'd heard that the village had never seen such cricket in years, and he had laughed till he cried!'

Lady Augusta turned away in disgust to her cool walk home across the park, and found herself stopped again by little Lady Windover, her eyes sparkling under her pretty hat.

"My dear Lady Augusta, what a *very* nice person Charles has grown into!" she cried. "I am absolutely *fascinated* by him! Leonard is asking him to dinner tomorrow night: he couldn't close his eyes for a moment during the sermon this morning!" She gave a wicked little laugh. "I was watching him all the time! You must be very proud of your young cousin, Lady Augusta. But it's a pity he's unmarried. I shall have to look about me and see if I can't find him a charming little wife while he is here. . . ."

And she went on to her carriage, leaving Lady Augusta to walk home with her two daughters and Major Goodyer, whose plea of a violent headache that morning, brought on by the heat, had not been permitted to let him off the duty of accompanying Ellen to church.

The engagement had been announced, his ring was on her finger, and the congratulations that had begun to pour in upon them were hollow enough to determine her to exhibit her fiancé to the village and to her friends.

There were some among them who commented unkindly that as Ellen was on the wrong side of thirty she couldn't afford to pick and choose, and others who said that no doubt the fortune she had inherited had come in handy, if it was only a husband that she was after, as it would take a lot of gold to cover the pill that was Ellen, while the villagers shook their heads and said sadly that if the old Squire had been alive she would never have dared bring a creature like that there Major Goodyer to the house, but that it was well known that Miss Ellen and her ladyship never did get on well together.

"I must say I cannot help feeling sorry for Lady Augusta to be forced to welcome such a son-in-law into the family," said Lady Gregson to Mrs. Harrison, as they watched the backs of the Manor party moving away across the park. "He's a terrible bounder, isn't he? I gave Ellen credit for more taste." Her ladyship was an old friend.

"My dear, Ellen isn't a girl. She has made up her mind to marry Archie Goodyer, and marry him she will," said Emily, but she didn't sound happy about it either, and she went on sadly, "It is all fixed up, the wedding is to be in two months' time, and the Major has given her an expensive-looking ring as a token of his affection."

"Which, no doubt, like the rest of it all, is quite worthless," said Lady Gregson, drawing down her mouth. "Poor Ellen. I've never liked her as much as I like Josey, but I'm sorry for her now."

And that, taking it by and large, was the opinion of most of the Harrobys' friends. Poor Ellen had done what she could to get herself a husband, and helped by her money and the Crabb-Taylors, who had never been noted for their brains, she had succeeded. Through Crabb the

Major had a nodding acquaintance with most of the neighborhood, and, although he had been cold-shouldered in the past, he was now accepted for Lady Augusta's sake.

And whatever was the actual worth of the ring on Ellen's finger it certainly looked very large and beautiful, while the Major, freed for the first time from the fear of mounting debts, became cocky enough to make all the Harrobys' male acquaintances long to kick him.

8

WHILE Ellen and her mother went to London to be fitted for wedding garments, to select a house suitable for Miss Harroby to rent, and to make arrangements for the wedding, Josey stayed at home to receive the small Julius Fanes when they arrived with their nurses.

The Major had accompanied Ellen to London, having plenty of arrangements to make on his own account in between squiring his fiancée and her mother, and Josey was glad to be rid of him. As long as she had been convinced that her sister saw him in the same light as she did herself she had not minded having him to stay in the house. But to contemplate him as a permanent member of the family was almost more than she could endure, and she could only pray that Ellen knew to the full what she was doing.

In the meantime, she showed herself well able to cope with the situation at home, however unexpected were the questions that suddenly arose.

There was, for instance, the incident of Winnie's youngest brother, who developed measles the day before the children were due to arrive.

"But of course Winnie must go home at once and stay there until the infection is over," Josey told Mrs. Grim. "We can't have poor little Julius exposed to infection of that sort! I suppose Winnie only found out about it when she went home yesterday?"

"Yes, Miss Josey, and I scolded her for it roundly. I didn't mince my words, I can tell you! 'Why ever did you go into the cottage, you silly girl?' I said. 'You knew that our children are coming here tomorrow. You'll probably go and catch measles yourself, or bring it to us on your clothes.' "

"Haven't we somebody else who would take Winnie's place in the nursery?" asked Josey. "What about one of the kitchen-maids? . . ."

"With all the extra work Cook will have on her shoulders I don't like to take either of them," said Mrs. Grim doubtfully. "But there's Polly . . . she's under-housemaid, and I dare say Doris could spare her. I'll have a word with Doris and see what we can arrange: she might have a younger sister who could come in temporary until Winnie comes back. Polly is a nice, clean girl, and so willing, as you know, Miss Josey. I don't suppose she'd make anything of taking hot water and trays up to the nursery between her other work."

"I'm sure she wouldn't," said Josey, relieved. She had a soft spot for Polly, who often waited on her when the maid she shared with Ellen was busy with her sister. "She's a pretty girl, with a gentle way that will be excellent with the children."

"Yes, Miss Josey." Mrs. Grim departed and sent for Polly to come to her room, where she told her that she would be required to take on Winnie's duties in the nursery for a time after the children arrived.

"I'll tell Doris to put some of the other girls on to doing your grates," she added. "There'll be the nursery fires to do every morning, you see, before you take the breakfast upstairs. I can't expect the nursery-maid to do that."

"No, of course not, Mrs. Grim."

"I hope that stupid Winnie will be back soon," said Mrs. Grim in an aggrieved tone. "It would be like her to catch the measles out of spite, with this wedding coming along and everything. Fancy sitting there and nursing the child on her knee, and him hot and feverish and with the rash full out on him! It was a mercy it wasn't scarlet fever!"

"Winnie is very devoted to her little brother, I know," said Polly. "She thinks the world of him and he of her. He was asking for her, poor little fellow."

"Well, he's got her now," said Mrs. Grim sourly. "I told her, I said: 'You needn't think you'll be on board wages, because you won't, my girl. You will go home and stay there until the doctor says it's safe for you to come back. And it's no good your mother thinking she'll be able to come here and fetch your wages at the end of the month, as she's been doing, because she's not to come near the house either."

Polly felt her heart wrung for Winnie's mother, who had been so pleased at getting her big, hungry girl into good service. One could only hope that the whole family would not go down with it, prolonging Winnie's enforced stay at home into months.

But in the meantime Polly enjoyed getting the nurseries ready for the small visitors and their nurses.

The rooms were situated on the second floor, just beneath the attics, and consisted of large day and night nurseries, with four more bedrooms for the nurses and older children.

The Julius Fanes' had two little girls and one precious boy, the youngest and the most delicate of the family. It was obvious that he must sleep with his nurse, Nurse Crampton, in the night nursery, while the little girls slept in the room next to Agnes, the nursemaid.

The dust-sheets were taken off the nursery furniture and the toys were brought out again and dusted and polished. The enormous dolls' house that had been made for a Harroby in the reign of George the Fourth, the old-fashioned rocking-horse, with one eye missing, the see-saw on its curved rocker, the high chair with the cane seat and the little rod thrust through the holes in the arms that looked far too flimsy to hold a child in check: all these things had to be brought from their store-room and dusted and polished. The cot was brought out too, and the mattress aired, the fire-guard found in the cupboard at the top of the stairs, with the bath and the nursery screen, covered in faded scraps.

Druggets were taken up from the carpets, the carpets swept with tea-leaves, the floors beneath scrubbed, and the paint washed down. Clean curtains were put up at the windows, candles and lamps were trimmed by old Burke and placed in readiness on high brackets where small hands could not reach them, and the clock on the mantelpiece was set going again after twenty years. And the estate carpenter, an old crony of Burke's, came in with his bag of tools and spent a whole morning making the gate safe at the top of the nursery stairs.

And as the warm air came in at the open windows, and the pigeons crooned at each other from the eaves above, Polly raised her head from her labors to peep out at the green world beyond the windows, and to think that no place in the world could be half as beautiful as Windover.

Looking down at the park with its trees and grazing cattle, at the white pony dragging the mower over the lawns, at the even rows of vegetables in a walled garden to the right, at the distant glory of the roses in a rose-garden to the left, she felt that she never wanted to leave it, and she envied the children who were to come to it so carelessly and casually, invited guests and members of the family that owned it.

"Come along, Polly! Don't stand there dreaming, my girl!" The head housemaid, Doris White, put her head in at the door. "There's all the blankets to take down and shake and put in the sun for a time. Nancy's got a bundle, and there is another bundle here for you. Pick them up and hurry, there's a good girl. There's plenty still to be done."

The moment had gone, the dreaming fled away. Polly ran to fetch the blankets and took them downstairs, and through the laundry to the drying-ground, where another under-housemaid, Nancy, was already shaking her bundle with the help of the laundry-maid, Sarah. Polly arranged her blankets beside theirs over the lines in the yard and was about to follow Nancy upstairs again when James put his head in at the yard door on his way to the stables. He stopped when he saw Polly, as he always did, although it pleased her sometimes to pretend that she hadn't seen him.

"What's this I hear, Polly?" he said. "Annie tells me you've been promoted again, this time to the nursery!"

She laughed at him over her shoulder, her eyes bright, her cheeks pink from shaking the blankets.

"Is it promotion?" she said with a little pout. "It's only

temporary work, James, nothing more. Not that I won't be glad to wait on the children, though I was thinking just now how much I envied them."

"Envied them?" He was puzzled, smiling down at her, and she went on quickly:

"Yes . . . to be able to come and live here at the Manor when and how they please, where everyone is sure to welcome them . . . where they can have everything they want. Mr. Charles was saying last Sunday that we are all equal, but it doesn't seem like that to me. These little children have so much, while my poor cousins at Moccrington scarcely have food to put into their mouths. I know my Aunt Ada says it's the will of Providence, but it does seem as if the Almighty's ways are a bit unfair at times, James. It don't seem quite right to me."

James frowned.

"Father says he don't hold with all that talk of equality and he doesn't think Mr. Charles ought to say such things, and him a Harroby. He says it's revolutionary stuff, and he's sorry to hear it spoken like that from the pulpit. The old Squire would turn in his grave. After all, Polly, my dear, the gentry aren't like us, whatever they may say or do, and Mr. Charles knows it. Isn't he one of them himself? So how can you or I be his equal? It isn't common-sensical."

"Oh, James!" She shook her head at him impatiently. "You don't understand, I expect, because you aren't educated, like Mr. Charles!" And then she ran off to fetch some more blankets, leaving him staring after her, still puzzled, and a little bit hurt.

Lady Augusta and Ellen had not returned by the time the day came for the children to arrive, and Josey asked Mrs. Harrison to have tea with her and help her to greet her small cousins.

"I don't want them to feel strange and unwanted, poor little things," she told Charles. "And with the Mater not here they might, you know."

Charles thought that if anybody could make children feel unwanted it would be his cousin Augusta, whose stiffness with young people was a byword in the family.

He remembered the treatment he had suffered at her hands when he was small and the relief with which he had escaped to the stables with Josey.

Lady Augusta believed that no child could be trusted not to get into mischief, that every child was naturally naughty, and if he told you he had been good he was almost certain to be lying. In her heart she disliked children, and they knew it, and were frightened of her in consequence, and would go to almost any length to avoid coming in contact with her.

But Mrs. Harrison was different: her face was gentle and kind, her blue eyes like a kitten's, innocent and trusting. She adored all children, and they adored her, and she spoilt them dreadfully, as Lady Augusta never hesitated to tell her.

"There is nothing worse than a spoilt child," she told Emily once, having caught her distributing sweets in the Sunday School. "I don't believe in bribing children, Emily. They should be taught to work for work's sake, and not for any reward. By giving them sweets you are inevitably *bribing* them to learn their Catechism."

Emily felt that they needed bribing, but she did not say so. It would have shocked Augusta to learn how sadly the Catechism bored her, both to learn and to teach to the young. Like sums, and French Grammar, and Geography, with all those parts colored pink where Great Britain ruled under the dear Queen. . . . Catechism was a boring sort of word, Emily thought: like a dry bun that stuck in your mouth and refused to be swallowed.

As she walked up to the Manor that afternoon her thoughts were not with the Sunday School or with the little Julius Fanes. She was thinking about Charles and his sermons, and she wished she could drop him a hint about the misgiving she was feeling without appearing to criticize. It was Augusta who liked to criticize, after all, and poor Charles had had enough of it from the lady of the Manor, without his cousin Emily starting on him as well. Charles, she found, was rather prickly these days, and did not take kindly to criticism, and one could not blame him for that.

It was a little disturbing, though, to see how people flocked to the little church every Sunday to hear him: one felt that so many of them might be inspired by curiosity and not much else . . . like that poem of Oliver Goldsmith's they had to learn years ago at school, something about "those who came to mock remained to pray." But she had not made up her mind yet whether Charles's congregation *did* remain to pray, and it worried her quite a lot.

So she held her tongue about the sermons and instead she talked about the state of the grass in the park, and how, if the dry weather continued, it would soon be ready for cutting for hay. And from there she went on to Josey and how well she was managing everything in her mother's absence, and that it all showed she was not nearly such a thoughtless hoyden as people liked to make out.

"But I've never thought Josey a hoyden," said Charles, surprised. "She's one of my best friends, and I admire her tremendously in spite of her looks. It's not her fault that she's like a good-looking monkey."

"I suppose it's her eyes that make one think she's like a monkey," said Emily thoughtfully. "In spite of her way of laughing at everything, her eyes are always sad."

"And are the eyes of monkeys sad, too?" he asked, teasing her.

"Always," she said seriously. "That is why I never like going into the monkey-house at the Zoo."

"My poor, conscience-stricken cousin!" He tucked her hand into his arm and kept it there. "*You* did not put them into their cages!"

"No, but by paying money to go and see them I may help to keep them there! . . . We must hurry, Charles. I can see Josey watching for us from the window of the little drawing-room and the carriage will be here in a few minutes now."

The children were to arrive by the afternoon train and a carriage had been sent to fetch them, one of the carts going on ahead for the luggage and the perambulators.

Tea was therefore to be at four-thirty instead of four

o'clock, and when Emily and Charles arrived they found Josey waiting for them in the little drawing-room that opened on to the rose-garden. A table was set out daintily in front of the long windows, and Josey greeted them warmly, with a glance of mischief for Charles.

"I had a letter from the Mater this morning," she said. "She expressed a hope that your sermons would not be too provocative while she is away."

"Charles is an idealist," said Emily uneasily.

"And the world is not kind to such people! You had better think again, Charles! You will either be locked up as a lunatic, or you will be banished to far-away places."

"That would suit me very well," he replied gravely. "The continual atmosphere of ladies' drawing-rooms is too suffocating for me."

"I am sorry I invited you in here, then, if it threatens to suffocate you. Would you prefer tea in the smoking-rooms? I have only to ring the bell and it shall be done. . . ."

He smiled down at her.

"You know I did not mean that," he said. "As if any atmosphere could be suffocating with you around, Josey!"

"Now am I to take that as a compliment or not?" She appealed to Mrs. Harrison. "Aunt Emily, did he imply that I am like an open window and likely to give everyone stiff necks, or does he simply mean that I'm like an east wind, blowing clean through the house and banging all the doors? If it is a compliment, I think it's a very back-handed one!"

"But I would not dream of insulting your intelligence by paying you compliments, Josey!" he said.

The laughter died from her face. "No," she said quietly, "I don't think you would." And he suddenly saw what Emily had meant when she said that Josey's eyes were sad. The next moment however she was rattling on: "Have you made up your mind what you are going to do, Charles, when you leave Windover in September? Are you planning to join your friend in the London slums, or are you going out among the heathen with a bible in your hand, teaching them to love their neighbors and giving them a good clout if they don't happen to want to love them after all?"

He shook his head.

"I'm afraid I'm not saint enough to battle against the odds as Raymond is doing in London, and I hold the reprehensible view that the black man should be left to enjoy his country and his life in his own way—evil and cruel though that may be, according to our standards."

"Then what are you going to do?"

He hesitated. "I'd like to go to one of the Colonies where our own people have settled—to Australia, or New Zealand, or to Canada, where the areas are vast and churches are few, and parsons badly needed. . . . I'd like to have hours in the saddle, and perhaps a bit of shooting now and then, and some fishing in the big lakes—" He broke off. "Why are you laughing at me?"

"Was I laughing? How rude of me! I was only thinking that there spoke the real Charles. You never wanted to go into the Church, did you?"

He shrugged his shoulders, annoyed with her for her laughter and for her astuteness.

"Your father insisted, and as he was kind enough to take me off my mother's hands, who was I to express an opinion?"

"You have dodged the question! That is what Archie Goodyer does, and I don't like it! But never mind. I think I can hear the carriage in the drive. . . ."

They hurried out to meet the children, and Josey ran down as the carriage drew up at the bottom of the steps and hugged them one by one as they were handed out to her, and kept young Julius on her arm while Nurse Crampton followed with Agnes.

And seeing her there, with delight on her face and her mouth smiling tenderly at the little boy as she bore him up the steps ahead of the nurses, Charles wondered again why Josey had never married, and what her male acquaintances were about that they could not see for themselves, as he had always seen, what an extremely nice and splendid person his cousin Josey could be.

Then, conscious of a pair of eyes on him, he turned his

head, and promptly Josey and the children went from his mind.

In the entrance hall, behind the butler Harris, Mrs. Grim stood waiting to conduct the nurses and their charges to the nurseries, where a large tea of bread-and-butter, and blackberry-and-apple jam, and sponge cakes, was set out for them on the square table in the day nursery. And beyond the housekeeper, standing in the shadows of the big hall, Charles saw a maid waiting to help with the children too, and as their eyes met and she gave him a little smile he saw that it was Polly.

She was astonishingly pretty, even with her lovely hair crowned by a hideous cap, and as she saw him staring at her she blushed a little, which made her prettier still. Now if Josey had a face like that, he thought, how different things might have been. . . .

And seeing him there in his clergyman's sober clothes, Polly thought again how young he looked after the old Rector. Why, he was almost like a schoolboy still, and with a schoolboy's eager, friendly ways. In spite of all that James had said, he had smiled at her just now as if she were his equal . . . and look at him now, teasing that starchy nurse and making her smile. . . .

The silver trays and the hot-house peaches, the footmen behind the chairs of the grand ladies' maids, the dinners in the stewards' rooms, the glory and the glamor that surrounded the great families of England in their stately homes, suddenly began to fade a little, and, in some unaccountable way, lost some of their fascination. . . .

9

IF it had been Ellen who had been left alone at the Manor while she and Josey went to London, Lady Augusta would have suggested that they should invite some older female relative to come and stay with her in their absence, to be her companion and chaperon. But Josey stood in no need of such companionship or chaperonage, and when her mother asked if they should not ask Emily Harrison to desert Charles for a few weeks, leaving him to the mercies of old Martha until she and Ellen returned, Josey had replied with spirit that Charles was in far greater need of a chaperon than she was.

"Lady Windover pursues the poor lad from morning until night," she said. "He is quite glad of the excuse of a funeral or a wedding or a baptism to free him from the bevy of young women she has at Broughton Park for his inspection. And in spite of Aunt Emily's co-operation and poor Charles's efforts I doubt if he will escape matrimony until the autumn. Lady Windover's young females make me ashamed of my own sex: a man has only to hand one of them a cup of tea for her to imagine that his intentions must be serious! It would be delivering Charles into the hands of the Philistines indeed if we left him at the Rectory for even a week without a keeper!"

"That, my dear," her mother said, "is rather vulgar."

"But then I am vulgar, am I not?" said Josey, unruffled. She smiled at her mother affectionately. "Poor Mater! It's hard on you to have such a daughter. You ought to have sent me back to the shop and exchanged me for a nice, healthy boy!"

While in London the ordering and fitting of wedding garments was taking up most of the time and attention of

Lady Augusta and her elder daughter, Ellen managed to snatch an afternoon here and there to pay some visits to her old benefactress's lawyer, Mr. Pierce, in Lincoln's Inn Fields. She did not take her future husband into the lawyer's offices with her: on the occasions when he accompanied her she left him to smoke a cigar in the carriage outside, feeling no doubt that the business she had with Mr. Pierce was private and entirely her own affair.

Down in Windover the children settled into the new quarters with the ease of the family of an officer in Her Majesty's Army. They were accustomed to furnished houses as they moved about from one place to another in the wake of the regiment. Often Nurse Crampton was left behind with them while their parents went abroad, and often they were left in furnished rooms, or with relatives, for months at a time.

But however often they moved, and wherever they went, Nurse Crampton never left them, and she became such a solid and unfailing factor in their lives that they could not imagine a world without her. No matter how often nursery-maids came and went, firm as a rock and equally immovable, she was there, to push the perambulator up hill and down dale, to dose them with medicines and grey powders, to induce them to eat milk pudding and prunes, to nurse them when they were sick and scold them when they were naughty, and to take them to church with her every Sunday.

She was in fact so much the rock on which their existence depended that when the choir sang "The Church's One Foundation" in church her charges felt that it must be connected, in some mysterious way, with Nurse. She was as enduring as the stars, and as dependable as birthdays and Christmas.

The two little girls were delighted to find the old-fashioned toys in the Windover nursery, and the scraps on the screen were a constant source of wonder to them as they were always discovering new pictures under the varnish on sleepy afternoons when they were made to rest, with the screen between their beds so that they would not talk.

Old Peters was brought out of his retirement in the almshouses and dressed up in his old livery, and the antiquated harness that belonged to the white pony was fetched out, with a large saddle, and it was brought round every morning for Peters to give the elder of the little girls, Susan, a riding lesson in the park, her smaller sister Miriam watching enviously from the terrace beside little Julius in his wicker perambulator.

And when Susan returned to Nurse Crampton to boast of her achievements she would say, her dark eyes smiling under her black sailor hat: "That's enough of that, Miss Vanity, if you please! Go on talking like that and you'll fall off next time you go riding, and then what will your father say?"

It was Nurse Crampton who took instant command of the situation when the nursery-maid Agnes fell down the back stairs and broke her wrist.

"She'd better go home until it's mended, Mrs. Grim," she said. "She's an awkward, clumsy girl, and I'm not surprised that she went and fell down like that. She never looks where she is going. But what's done can't be undone, and it's no use crying over spilt milk."

"But you can't manage without a nursery-maid, Nurse!" Mrs. Grim was concerned for her. "Would you like me to make enquiries in the village, in case I can find a likely girl to help you while Agnes is away? If I could manage without a still-room maid I'd offer you Mary while her ladyship is still away, but with this wedding coming along I dare not be without her, though I know how fond the children are of her."

"They are fonder of the cakes she makes!" said Nurse with a sniff. "No, Mrs. Grim, you can keep Mary and welcome. The girl I would like, if you can spare her, is one of the under-housemaids—that nice Polly Kettle—and let you find somebody else from the village to help with the trays and the hot water and so on. I can't be too careful with Master Julius after that terrible illness of his last winter, and all brought on by that stupid Maud taking him out in his pram in the middle of the winter without a hat on! We nearly lost him, you know, thanks to Maud, as

I told her when I sent her packing. 'It's no good crying and carrying on,' I said. 'If he was lying dead in his coffin at this moment, poor mite, it would be all your fault, and no amount of tears would bring him back.' There was straw down in front of the house for weeks, ankle deep, and the door-knocker done up in a kid glove ... I thought I'd never have another peaceful night."

Mrs. Grim, while sympathizing over the delinquent Maud, refrained from remarking that she had no very high opinion of Agnes, either. She thought she was far too flighty for a children's maid. Had she not caught her with Albert in the dark of the back stairs more than once, and was she not always making excuses to go out in the stable yard, just to see if James was there?

"Polly is certainly a very nice girl," she agreed. "And she loves children. You might do worse than have her to look after the little girls for a time. I'll speak to her about it at once, Nurse."

And so Polly became nursery-maid at the Manor, with the lightest work she had known so far in her eighteen and a half years. She dressed the two little girls and washed them and undressed them, and saw them into bed at night: she read to them and sewed for them and brushed the tangles out of their curls and took them for walks in the park and the village. She washed their pinafores and starched and ironed them, and washed the baby's frocks and her own and Nurse's caps and aprons.

Sleeping alone now in the room next to theirs, Polly found her dreams subtly changing. The silver trays and the footmen and the champagne were fading into a fairy tale that she had been told by somebody long ago, when she was still only a child. It was becoming more and more unreal now that she was growing up, and she found herself dreaming instead of a day when she might be head nurse in a big household, with willing feet to run for her and willing hands to do her bidding, and small and lovely children to look after and to love.

As they sat over their meals together in the nursery after the children had done, or sewed by the light of the nursery lamp in the evenings, Nurse Crampton told her of households where there were footmen to wait on the nurseries, not great hobbledehoys like Albert, but grand young men with powdered hair.

"And very nasty it is too, that powdered hair," went on Nurse severely. "I'm glad it is going out of fashion nowadays. The poor fellows go about nearly all day with wet heads, because first of all they have to wet their hair, and then they have to rub the soap into a stiff lather, and then the powder is put on top of that! Enough to give them their death, I always say, and it all has to be washed out every night and the hair oiled after—a nasty, messy business—though I must say it looks nice with the colored coat of a smart livery, it's no use saying it doesn't. I remember," she went on, "when I was nurse to the Marquis of Woodhouse's children: little Lord Crowborough and his sisters, Lady Juliet and Lady Ruth. I had two footmen to wait on me there, and two under-nurses besides the nursery-maid, and never the same food two days together. Very particular they were there about the nurses' food, just as particular as I was about the children's meals. I told the housekeeper, I said, 'Mrs. West,' I said, 'children are children and their stomachs are the same whether they be the children of an army officer or the children of a marquis or a duke. We may appreciate rich food, but children don't. They very easily get upset and bilious, and rice pudding is best for *my* nursery,' I said. But you should have seen the way the servants were treated there, Polly! We always had a Servants' Ball every Christmas, with champagne and a first-class buffet supper, and the house steward would dance with the Marchioness, and the Marquis would lead out Mrs. West for the first dance, and all the servants wore evening dress, just like the gentry. There were fifty indoor servants there, not counting the outside, gardeners and grooms and such. All the local tradespeople were invited, and it was held in the dining-room, which was cleared for the occasion, and a band hired from London, special." She sighed. "Ah well, I was a good bit younger in those days, Polly, and it was my first place as head nurse. . . ."

Polly listened dreamily, as she sewed away at the little girls' dresses in the lamplight, and then she looked across the nursery-table at Nurse Crampton, middle-aged, grey-haired, thick-set, and formidable, and she found it hard to imagine her a young girl like herself, and she wondered what she had gained from all those years of devoted service to other people's children.

She had their love and careless kisses for a fleeting space, a warm hug or two, the pride of knowing later how well they had done in the world, and that most of it was due to her strict, but loving upbringing, and then in the future there would be old age for her in an almshouse, like poor old Biddy Webb, with no child or grandchild to come near or to care. . . .

And Polly found that she did not want that sort of life for herself. Eventually she wanted her own home, with husband and children, but it was still a hazy sort of want in a dreamlike future, untouched by reality.

The young men at Windover who tried to court her made her laugh by their clumsy ways: there was Albert, who had been ready to share his kisses with Agnes after Polly had laughed at his advances, and there was the young gardener Bob, always smelling of earth and sweat and bonfires, and a young keeper or two, always out of a night. . . . Maybe she would have to wait until she was as old as Doris or Mary, or even Miss Edwards, or Emms, and marry a butler after all. . . .

So Polly planned her life, re-planning it the next moment with secret laughter, and a feeling of suppressed excitement, as if something wonderful was lurking round the next corner, something much more exciting than silver trays and champagne, something that was surely there, only waiting for her to find it. And of James as a possible suitor she did not think at all.

And then one day, after she had been acting as nursemaid at the Manor for about a fortnight, Nurse Crampton learned from a casual remark she made that she had not been to see either of her aunts for three months.

"But there was no call for me to go and see them, really, and I always have every third Sunday evening off," Polly said, smiling.

"And then you only go round to the Burkes' cottage!" said Nurse with a shake of her head. "Thanks must be where thanks is due. That's what I always say, and these aunts of yours that have brought you up do deserve to see you once in a while. So you take tomorrow afternoon off and go and see them, my dear, seeing that it's Wednesday and the middle of the week. I always let that Agnes go out for a Wednesday afternoon—not that she has ever rewarded me by working any harder afterwards! But I know you will, because you are a good, conscientious girl, Polly, and I like you, it's no good saying I don't. You go off tomorrow afternoon and see those good aunties of yours, and show them that hat Miss Josey gave you—the one with the daisies on the brim. It didn't suit her a bit, but it looks a treat on you. .... I'll manage the children, as long as you are back by six."

"I'll be back, Nurse," said Polly gratefully. "And thank you very much."

The following afternoon saw her starting off for the station in one of the Manor carts, driven by James, who promised that he would be at the station again later on that afternoon to meet the five o'clock train from Market Broughton.

"And don't you miss it, whatever you do," he added warningly. "Or it will be a long walk home for you. I can't meet the next, because Miss Josey wants me to take Mrs. Harrison over to Broughton Park."

"I won't miss it, James dear," said Polly, and as she got down at the station and stood for a moment beside him she added with a touch of coquetry and an upward glance: "You haven't said that you admired my hat! Don't you think it's a pretty one?"

"Very pretty," he replied, but his eyes were not on the hat but on the face beneath it, and seeing him like that gravely smiling and yet with something else in his face behind it all, for the first time Polly was embarrassed and wished that she had not drawn his attention to her hat, and hurried away to buy her ticket.

Until she reached the shop and saw the shutters up and remembered that it was early-closing day in Market Broughton, Polly had not given a thought to what she would do if her Aunt Hannah was not at home, and it was only after she had rung the bell at the side door three times that a neighbor put out her head and told her that her aunt was out for the day.

"Your Uncle Ebenezer was took bad," she said, the eyes beneath the curlpapers that ornamented her forehead regarding Polly and her hat with some curiosity. "Fell off his cart he did, one day last week, and the doctor says he thinks it was a stroke. But your aunt, she holds it was drink, and I dessay she's right, though why your poor uncle shouldn't have his pint like other folk I've never known. Anyway, he's been taken off to the hospital and your aunt said she'd go and spend the day with him, seeing as it's a nice day."

The nearest hospital to serve Market Broughton was fifteen miles away, at Ely, and Polly turned to look at the church clock, and saw that it was a quarter to three. She might be able to get out to her Aunt Ada's by half past if she had boots on her feet, but in her vanity she had changed them for a pair of shoes—also cast-offs of Miss Josey's, and a tiny bit too small for their present wearer. The thought of walking three miles in them and finding Aunt Ada out, because she often worked in the fields during the summer months, and then walking back again, and all in the heat of a warm day, was anything but inviting.

The afternoon, lovely and empty as the smiling landscape that surrounded the little town, was just so much wasted time on her hands. She could not go back before the appointed train, otherwise another long walk to the Manor would wait for her there, and feeling vexed and frustrated, she turned her back on the empty shop and walked on up the High Street, which was equally deserted that afternoon.

She looked at some of the garments in the windows where blinds had not been drawn down against the sun, and caught a reflection of herself in the pretty hat and the high-heeled shoes in the windows where the blinds were drawn, and strolled on with the warm sunshine beating on her shoulders under her thin blouse, until she found herself at the opening to Church Lane.

The church door was open and there was a seat in the porch that offered rest to her feet, and she made her way towards it. It was cool in the porch and quiet, except for the persistent cawing of the rooks in the Vicarage trees. And then, as she sat down on the seat, thinking about her Uncle Ebenezer and wondering what she could do to pass the long hours of the afternoon, there came brisk footsteps inside the church and the door behind her was opened, and Charles Harroby stepped out into the porch.

10

IT was queer, Polly thought later, how his presence there, unexpected as it was, became a perfectly natural answer to her wasted afternoon. In fact, in that first moment of meeting him, it seemed as if her aunt's shop might have been closed against her for this very purpose.

As for Charles, he stopped short, at first astonished and then obviously delighted to see her, as he always was when he met a friend, and he kept his hat in his hand instead of clapping it back on his head. He might have just taken it off to her, as if she had been a lady.

"Why, it's little Polly Kettle!" he exclaimed. "What are you doing here, pray, so far away from Windover?"

She explained about the unexpected holiday and the closed shop and her Uncle Ebenezer, and as she talked his eyes watched her face in much the same way as James's had done, although from time to time they shifted to the pretty hat and she wondered if he were trying to recall where he had seen it before, and she wished she had not worn it that afternoon. The plain black sailor, like Nurse Crampton's, would have been far more suitable.

As she stopped speaking, however, his eyes came back to her face and he said smilingly: "What a shame, to have your little holiday wasted in this fashion! But you should have let your aunt know that you were coming, and then she would not have gone off to the hospital to see your uncle today."

Polly shook her head.

"There wasn't time to write her a letter," she told him. "And if I had it would have made no difference. Not if she had made up her mind to see Uncle Ebenezer. Nothing shifts my Aunt Hannah once she has made up her mind."

"We both seem to suffer from strong-minded ladies in the family," said Charles, daringly, his eyes dancing a little. He sat down in the porch beside her. "When are you going back to Windover?"

"By the four-thirty train, Mr. Charles. James is going to meet me at the station at five."

"Is he, by Jove? He must have fallen under the spell of your pretty eyes, Polly! ... I had to argue a good hour before I could persuade old Herrick to perform a like service for me this afternoon. The horse was tired, he said, and there was the churchyard to be mown. 'Hang the churchyard,' I said. 'I'm not walking all those miles for any churchyard in England.' Old Herrick disapproves of me, I'm afraid."

"He disapproves of everybody, sir," said Polly. "He's a bad-tempered old busybody, is old Herrick. Everyone knows that."

"Do they, indeed?" he said. What a pretty creature she was, and what beautiful hair it was under that hat! He guessed it might be a cast-off from one of his cousins, and thought how right Josey had been when she had complained that all her hats looked so much prettier on the maids than they ever looked on her. Those pink-tipped daisies were the color of Polly's pink-and-white skin, the gold of the straw was almost the same shade as her hair, and the blue velvet ribbon matched her eyes. Here he pulled himself up abruptly and said in a cooler tone: "There are some interesting old tombstones in this churchyard, Polly. Have you ever looked at any of them?" He got up and she followed him obediently through the long grass, and tried to find an interest when he laughed at the quaint wording of some of the epitaphs, and was rather solemn about it because she had been brought up to think that one should not make fun of the dead.

The sun beat down more warmly than ever as they came to a large tomb that was enclosed by iron railings, the stone slab inside the railings so overgrown with moss and lichen and brambles that it was impossible to see any names that were inscribed on it.

Polly had taken off her hat and she was using it as a fan, and standing on the opposite side of the grave she leaned her arms along the railing, her eyes grave and her mouth solemn as she waited for him to find something to amuse and interest him there.

But Charles had momentarily forgotten the tombstones in that old churchyard. He was looking at Polly as if he had never really seen her before, and a half-forgotten tag of verse intruded itself upon his mind:

> "The Blessed Damozel lean'd out
> From the gold bar of Heaven
> Her blue grave eyes were deeper much
> Than a deep water, even.
> She had three lilies in her hand
> And the stars in her hair were seven. . . ."

Leaning there on that railing, with her grave face and eyes, she might indeed have been the Blessed Damozel of Rossetti's poem leaning on the gate of Heaven. He dragged his eyes from her with an effort, trying to remember Windover and his family and the difference in their situations, and he told himself not to be a fool.

"How warm it is!" he said abruptly.

"Yes, sir." She looked about her at the empty churchyard. "I wish there was a tea-shop where I could get a cup of tea." She had had an early lunch and a light one.

"Now that's a very good idea!" Charles caught at it eagerly. "There is a tea-shop in the High Street, though I doubt if it will be open on a Wednesday. But there is no harm in seeing, is there, Polly?"

He walked with her to the gate and out into the lane and down the lane into the High Street, and it was quite as empty as before. The tea-shop however was open, and Charles led the way to one of the small, marble-topped tables inside and ordered tea and cakes for himself and Polly.

He was fully aware that what he was doing was reprehensible and that if it should ever reach Lady Augusta's ears he would be asked to leave Windover at once. But he was in a reckless mood that afternoon, and he did not care a straw for Lady Augusta, and, in fact, he hoped that she would hear that he had given one of her housemaids a cup of tea in Market Broughton in broad daylight. He was rather sorry that it was early-closing day, and that there were not more people about to see him do it. About Polly herself and how such an escapade might affect her he did not think at all.

Over tea she lost a little of her shyness and told him about her aunts, and about her Uncle Ebenezer and the green-grocer's shop, and the servant her aunt had to wait on her, and he teased her about having grand relations just to see the pink come flooding into her face.

The time went so fast that it was time to catch the train back to Windover before they knew it, and Charles paid for their tea and escorted her to the station, and there, still in his reckless mood, instead of letting her get into a third-class compartment while he went off to find a first-class carriage for himself, he travelled with her, sitting opposite and pointing out various things to her as they went, and helping her down from the carriage when they stopped at Windover as if she had been Miss Josey.

"Goodbye, Polly," he said when they parted in the driveway outside the little station. "Thank you for a most charming afternoon." And he went off to the bad-tempered old Herrick and the Rectory gig while she went to find James and the Manor dog-cart.

"So Mr. Charles was on the train," said James, as they moved off after the gig.

"Yes," said Polly with a demure glance up at him from under the daisy-trimmed hat. She was glad that neither James nor old Herrick had seen them alighting from the same carriage. To be sure there was no harm in travelling in the same railway carriage with Mr. Charles, but she felt that such a journey, short as it was, might have been misunderstood. And from the same reason she did not mention their tea together in the High Street either, although she could not help remembering how handsome

Mr. Charles was, and what lovely manners he had, and the things he had said about her eyes over tea.

"Where did you get those eyes from, Polly?" he said, and then, as she lifted them, startled and shy, to his face, he had added a bit of poetry about deep water that she had not understood, but it sounded very beautiful all the same. She couldn't imagine James ever quoting poetry about her eyes. ... She glanced sideways at him as they jogged along through the lanes and she thought he was more stolid and silent than usual.

There was the scent of clover and cut hay in the fields, and the hedges were pink and white with wild roses. Supposing she had not been a maid, she thought, her heart giving a little twist under the thin white blouse: supposing she had been a lady born, and Mr. Charles had come talking poetry to her then? ... Would it have been the beginning of something else ... some wonderful, distant, scarcely-to-be-thought-of dream?

Her thoughts having wandered far away from the dogcart and James, she did not notice that he was pulling up by the side of the road until he came to a standstill. The Rectory gig was almost out of sight, and James waited until it had turned the corner and the road ahead was empty, before he put his hand on hers, crashing in on the cobweb quality of her dreaming.

"Polly," he said, speaking more slowly than usual and with some difficulty in choosing his words. "I've wanted to ask you this for a long time ... but there never seems to be an opportunity ... and walking home with you Sunday evenings seems like putting you under an unfair disadvantage, somehow. ... But Polly, my dear, if you could ever see your way to marrying me I'd be the happiest chap alive." He did not give her time to answer, but went on as if he had thought it all out in his slow way: "There's opportunities these days for chaps like me, if they've a way with horses. Once this wedding of Miss Ellen's is over, Briggs says he doesn't think her ladyship will keep more than one groom besides the stable-boy, and that's not what I want, Polly. I've got it in mind to try for another post—as coachman in a great gentleman's house-

hold, and if you'd say yes I'd make a real set at it, so I
would. There'd be a cottage, you see, and the money
would be better, because I'd never take you to anything
that wasn't good enough for you, my dear—" He suddenly saw that she was staring at him with open dismay
and he broke off. "What is it, Polly? Why are you looking
at me like that?"

"Oh!" said Polly indignantly. "Oh, James, how can you
be so silly? If I'd thought you were going to talk like this
I'd have walked from the station, shoes or no shoes!"

The light died out of James's face and it went suddenly
still.

"I don't see that it's silly," he said quietly, "to ask a girl
to marry you."

"But of *course* it's silly!" cried Polly. "When it's *you*
... and me! Why, you've been a good friend to me for
years, James, and I never dreamed as you'd spoil it all in
this way. Who have I got to go to when I want help, now
you've turned on me like this?"

"Turned on you?" He was puzzled and hurt. "Polly,
what do you mean?"

"I mean this," she said, almost crying with disappointment. "You are no better than that stupid Albert, always
wanting to kiss me round corners! ... How can I come to
your home of a Sunday with this between us? You've
spoilt everything, James!"

The puzzlement left James's eyes, leaving a queer,
rough tenderness there instead.

"But Polly, my little love," he said gently, "just because
you know now that I love you and want to marry you,
that's no call for you to feel any different towards me,
surely? I'm still your friend, just as I've always been, and
if so be as you don't feel you can love me yet awhile, then
don't go imagining things will be any different between us,
my dear. Because I'm still here, and I'm still the same old
James as I always was, and, until you ask me to, I swear
I'll never speak a word of this to you again!" He squeezed
the little hands under his big one and then took it away,
and gathering up the reins he drove on, looking ahead of
him.

Her conscience woke up then, and she stole a timid glance at him from time to time to see if he looked put out or angry, but he was unruffled and calm, and presently she took heart and put her hand on his knee and said in an ashamed little voice:

"I'm sorry, James, if I was unkind. I didn't mean to be. It is very nice of you to feel like you do about me, and I'm truly grateful ... but I don't want to marry anybody."

His eyes remained steadily on the white road ahead of them, where a small cloud of dust vanishing over the brow of the next hill was all that remained of the Rectory gig. The hand on his knee might not have been there, and after a moment she took it away.

"I understand, Polly," he said then. "Don't worry your head any more about stupid old James. We'll forget that he ever talked the nonsense he did, shall we?"

"Let's!" said Polly eagerly, but somehow she could not forget, and from that evening, although outwardly James was unaltered, gentle, silent, and kind, the elder brother and the friend of years, a small and rather unworthy feeling of triumph would possess her when she thought about him. There was, in fact, a naughtiness in her smile and a provocation in her eyes when they met that would have angered him if it had not given him some measure of hope, because he could see that his little Polly was finding her feet and beginning to grow up.

But the part that Charles Harroby was to have in that growing up he could not in the least imagine.

"I think Anna will be the one," said Lady Windover positively. "I really think she will ... he has just played his third game of tennis with her, and I saw him smiling into her eyes. In England that almost amounts to a proposal of marriage, you know!"

"What on earth are you talking about, my love?" said her husband indulgently. "Who smiled into Anna's eyes? Not that I blame the fellow, because she's got very pretty eyes ... almost as pretty as yours!"

"Now, Leonard!" His wife pouted. "You know I'm talking about Charles Harroby. . . ."

"Oh—ah, yes. The curate! I wonder what there is about a curate—especially a good-looking one—that sends otherwise intelligent women off their heads."

"Now, Leonard, don't pretend that you don't like him, darling!"

"I like him very much. He's a good chap in his way and a first-class cricketer. But give me old Lionel's sermons before his! A fellow could sleep through those without hindrance. Charles makes it impossible for anybody to sleep. . . . Damn it, you never know what he's going to come out with next!" He sounded justly indignant and Lady Windover smiled.

"I am sure that Anna will be just the right wife for him. She is quite wrapped up in good works. Aunt Trudie said she worked like a black for that mission in the East End—the one where Miss Mackenzie's nephew is Curate. She went down there twice a week for a whole month, and Aunt Trudie said they quite adored her."

"Including the Curate? And was that why she went?"

"Leonard! What a thing to say! She went to distribute clothing for the Mission, and milk for the babies, and . . . to bring a little sunshine into grey lives."

"And did the curate enjoy it as much as the recipients of all these good works?"

"I don't know anything about the curate, except that he was Miss Mackenzie's nephew, and that she runs the Mission for him, but Aunt Trudie—who is Miss Mackenzie's greatest friend—told me that the poor creatures just *lived* for Anna's visits, and she was very sorry when Anna had to give it up."

"Still, they—and the curate—had eight visits to look back on—as sunshine to gild all those drab lives, and what more could they ask? That should console Anna—and Miss Mackenzie's nephew—a great deal."

And Lord Windover went off to talk to the pretty Anna, whom he regarded as more than a bit of a minx.

Lady Windover and her sister Anna had shared the considerable fortune that had been left them by their

grandfather, an American dollar millionaire, and while
Lady Windover had married and settled down at
Broughton Park in complete happiness, her sister was still
unmarried. The truth was that Anna had a poor opinion
of the British aristocracy, and no desire to buy herself a
title, and only recently had her romantic mind been cap-
tured by Charles Harroby's looks and careless disregard
for her fortune. While his light-hearted manner implied
that she was a very charming little person for a mild flirta-
tion, and to pass the hours of a rather tedious summer, he
appeared to refuse to take her seriously and this piqued
Anna not a little.

"Charles Harroby," she had observed to her sister
rather unwisely once, "is a man that I could marry." And
naturally Lena Windover decided that marry him she
should.

Was not Broughton Rectory much smaller and more
manageable than Windover, and was not the living in her
husband's gift? With Anna's money the old house could
be made into a beautiful and comfortable dwelling, because it had only twenty bedrooms where Windover had
thirty, and three acres of garden where Windover Rectory
had four.

Charles soon became as fully aware of Miss Anna's
pursuit of himself as he was of Lady Windover's kind
intentions on his behalf. He could not move a yard outside
Windover nowadays without running into pretty girls,
most of them being sponsored by Lena Windover, and he
found himself clinging to Josey's side on these occasions
and imploring her with mock alarm not to desert him.

Most of the girls to whom he was introduced that summer were looking out for husbands, while as for Anna,
though he did not under-rate her determination, he was
equally determined that wild horses—and Lena Windover—would not drag him to the altar.

"I shall accept no invitations in future when you have
not been invited as well," he told Josey one day soon after
the Broughton Park tennis party. "I need protection,
Josey! Do you know that Lena is talking about the
Broughton Park living again?"

"I shouldn't worry about that, Charles. She has been talking about it ever since she came here, and Leonard is much too indolent to do anything about it. As long as we have a rector in Windover he is not going to bother to open up his vicarage at Broughton. They haven't had a vicar there for years."

"Nevertheless, the next time I go to Broughton Park I shall ask if I may bring you with me," said Charles. "I will take you and bring you back in my gig, and I will never leave your side while we are there!"

"Then you will have people saying that *we* are enjaged," said Josey composedly. "And that would be worse still!"

"On the contrary," he replied. "I could think of many worse fates than that!"

She tried to laugh, but her eyes did not meet his.

"Take care!" she warned him. "One pretty speech like that to Anna and you are a lost man!"

The following afternoon as he was taking a short cut through the park from Windover Common he ran into Miss Anna, who was so naively surprised to see him there that he did not remember having told her once that this was his favorite walk.

"This is an unexpected pleasure!" he said, replacing the straw boater that was Lady Augusta's despair on the back of his head after the manner of a Sixth Form schoolboy. Lady Augusta liked clerical garments to be as orthodox as possible on the curate-in-charge, and did not at all approve of the liberties the young man took with his headgear as well as his jackets. The tweed suits that he wore during the week were even worse than the flannels and the blazer that he wore for playing tennis. "Are you walking over to the Manor?"

"No. I was going to see Mrs. Harrison." Her eyes rested on him admiringly, as she thought how handsome he was. "She wanted some of our American recipes for preserves, and I promised to lend her this book." She held out a slim volume. "It was such a lovely day that I decided to walk instead of having the carriage."

"A lovely day indeed," he assented gravely. She stole

another look at his face and her heart began to beat a little faster. Was it possible, she wondered, to induce this aloof young man to make love to her? And what would he be like if he did? There was a hint of hidden fire about Charles Harroby that made any exploration of his nature interesting and exciting.

"A penny for your thoughts!" she said, after they had walked on for some yards in complete silence.

He laughed a little self-consciously. "I am sure you would not find them worth your pennies!" he protested.

"Nevertheless, I'd like to know them," she said with a swift upward glance. "I'm not a butterfly like my sister, Mr. Harroby ... I have serious thoughts myself sometimes."

His eyes began to twinkle in a way that made her feel a little uncomfortable.

"I was wondering," he said deliberately, "if there was a good cure for bunions. ..."

"For—" She gasped. "I *beg* your pardon?"

"I am sorry," he apologized, seeing that she was offended. "But you *did* ask me what I was thinking about. ... I have just come from visiting one of my parishioners, a poor old man on the Common, which is about two and a half miles from the village itself. As long as his feet could transport him there, his only interest was in walking that two and a half miles to the Harroby Arms and back again. But now, alas, his bunions are so bad that he can scarcely put his foot to the ground to walk one mile, let alone five!"

She was shocked. "And so you would find him a cure for his bunions just so that he can go that distance to waste his money in drinking?" she said indignantly.

"Please," he begged her, "don't sound like my cousin Augusta! That is exactly how the problem would appear to her! No doubt if I wanted to get him to church, one of the traps from the Manor might be put at his disposal now and then. But to get poor old Zachy to the public house, where most of his old cronies forgather of an evening, talking of old times and exchanging local gossip—that would be out of the question. And how could I, a parson, think of such a thing? If the old man feels lonely and cut off from his world, hasn't he got his Bible to read and a goat to talk to? What more can he want?"

She was chagrined at his teasing and annoyed because she felt that he had put her in the wrong, when of course she had been absolutely in the right. They had reached the entrance to a little coppice of trees, cool and shady, and she put down her parasol and poked with its pointed ferrule at the heads of the wild parsley, waist deep under the trees on either side of the path.

"I hope you took him some rum to console him," she said drily.

"I took him some home-brewed beer, which was better, and shag for his clay pipe, and the latest village gossip to amuse him. And I promised I would speak to the house-keeper at the Manor about his bunions. There is practically nothing that Mrs. Grim doesn't know about foot troubles."

She turned her head and met his laughing eyes with a petulant little pout. She was not accustomed to young men who found bunions an interesting subject when they were in her company, and she began to wonder if she were wise to encourage him. She thought that her Aunt Trudie might not approve of him at all.

"That must have comforted him a great deal, but I should have thought it would have been possible to arrange with some farmer and his wife to fetch him to church in their trap on Sundays."

"But Zachy is a great deal older than I am, and he has reached an age now when a man must accept things or die with doubt in his heart. Zachy has accepted without question so much as being God's will—much that in his place I would have questioned fiercely and set my face against until the end. But he does not do so because his faith has a simplicity that mine lacks. I know myself to be so much less a Christian than he is that it is quite impossible for me to go to him and say, "Zachy, you have got to come to church to hear me preach!" I may be a hypocrite, Miss Anna, but not so deep a one as that!"

He had forgotten his companion and was speaking his

thoughts aloud, as he spoke them to Josey and to Emily, and her annoyance deepened.

"He sounds a most disagreeable old man," she said tartly, and her brittle voice recalled him to the coppice, and the sunlight and shade of that pleasant path, and he was hunting about for something to say that would not shock her any further when two small girls came flying down the path towards them, pursued by a hatless young woman.

The children were laughing as loudly as she was, and they were only brought up at last by the two people that barred their way, all three equally out of breath.

"It's Cousin Charles!" cried the bigger of the children, Susan, smiling up at him rapturously and clasping him round the knees. "Oh, Cousin Charles, why did you stop us? We'd got Polly's hat and we were going to throw it in the lake. . . ."

"Then it's just as well that I did stop you!" He unclasped her arms and picked up the black sailor hat with its long hatpins from where she had thrown it and handed it back to Polly. Her hair had escaped from some of its pins and was blowing into her eyes, her face was flushed with running and her lips were parted, and she looked very pretty indeed. "Here you are, Polly!" he said, smiling. "You'd better put it on again while you have the chance!"

"Thank you, sir!" She put it on hastily, jabbing the hatpins through the golden curl of a bun on top of her head. "Come along, dears. We've got to go home to tea." She took the children's hot little hands firmly in hers and turned back up the path.

Anna said: "What a pretty nursemaid! She must cause quite a flutter up at the Manor among her rustic beaux!" They came out into the park and she put up her sunshade against the rays of the sun. "Oh dear, how hot it is! I rather wish I had come in the carriage after all!"

"Let me walk with you up to the Manor," he said, suddenly anxious to be rid of her. "It isn't as far as the Rectory and Josey will give you tea and send you back to Broughton in the carriage."

She glanced up at him from under the shade of her

frilly hat. "And you?" she said softly. "Will you come with me, Mr. Harroby?"

He made the excuse of cricket practice on the green that evening, and he saw her mouth droop and the peevish look come back to her eyes, and after he had left her with Josey he went on with her book of recipes to the Rectory, and sat down at old Lionel Harroby's writing-table in the study and stared out through the long windows that opened on to the lawn.

There was a scent of roses coming from the climbing damask rose outside, and bees, drunk with honey, came blundering round the stocks that were just coming into bloom in the borders beneath. Emily was having tea with Lady Gregson, and he had left Anna's book on the hall table for her to see when she came in, and in shutting the study door upon it he shut out the thought of Anna too. He found her tiresome and troublesome, and he wished that she would leave him alone. Did she think he was another Archie Goodyer, ready to pursue a woman for the sake of a comfortable life on her money?

With his elbows resting on the table where Lionel had written his scholarly sermons, and with his hands gripping each other lightly, he sat and scowled at the lawn that had been his old cousin's pride. He was tired of Lady Augusta and her friends, he was sick to death of girls like Anna. The only girl whose little finger was worth more than the lot of them was his cousin Josey, and Josey was . . . Josey. Happy as he always was in her company he did not dream of thinking of her in any other light except as a cousin and a friend. Perhaps the best friend that he had ever had. . . .

He longed to get away from England with its petty barriers of class to a country where life was less restricted, and where a man's future was what he made it and neither more nor less.

Josey might laugh at him and call him a Radical or a Socialist if she liked, but he knew himself to be a misfit before anything. His mother wept over him and said it was all the fault of "that horrid Oxford," but when he treated Emily to some of his wild talk she only smiled and said that it didn't do to run your head against a brick wall.

"You ought to find some nice young woman, dear, and marry and settle down," she told him serenely. "It would change your outlook on life wonderfully."

But whom could he find to share a future that was so uncertain? Not Anna, with her spoilt, pretty smile and her flawless complexion, and her lovely, expensive gowns. A pioneer's wife could not ride about in carriages with lace parasols held up to protect her face from the sun. . . .

And as he sat there thinking and dreaming, his thoughts went back suddenly to a girl whose face had been sunburnt and flushed with running, with untidy corn-coloured hair curling about her face, and a slender young figure in a dress of white piqué . . . a girl who had leaned on the railings of an overgrown tomb in a country churchyard, like the Blessed Damozel leaning on the bar of Heaven. . . .

And then, startled at where his wayward thoughts were leading him, he pulled himself up and groaned aloud, and picked up the pen with which old Lionel had written his sermons from the desk and held on to it as if it were a straw, and he a drowning man. . . .

Until, like a straw, it snapped in his hands.

11

Winnie's little brother recovered from the measles and none of the rest of the family caught it. She came back to her duties at the Manor a little thinner than when she left it, and was dismayed to find that Polly had been whisked away from her to the nursery, and that Nancy was to share her room instead.

"Never mind," Polly said. "Nancy is nice to work with, though she is a bit particular—more than I used to be! But she'll teach you more in a day than I'd teach you in a week, so you are lucky to have her."

Winnie was not overwhelmed by her good fortune.

"She's as thick as thieves with Doris," she grumbled. "And you know what Doris is—always at you, nag, nag, nag! 'Pick up that duster now, you haven't polished those taps, take a duster, not your apron . . . do this, do that, and be quick about it!' That's Doris—and Nancy will be the same."

"Do you good!" said Polly, laughing, and went back to the nursery.

The little girls, Susan and Miriam, had grown so fond of her that she had to be careful not to arouse Nurse Crampton's jealousy. They liked it best when she took them for a walk, and they went down to the woods, to race about until they were tired, when they would be glad to sit quietly with her on an old tree-trunk, Polly with an arm about each, while she read to them from their book of *Grimms' Fairy Tales*. The warm, sweet smell of them, their engaging ways, their soft hair blowing across her cheek like strands of silk, the feel of their crisp muslin frocks with the fine smocking that Nurse was teaching her to do in the evenings, their very way of taking for granted

She's one of the under-housemaids, and she's a very nice girl. She maids me sometimes when Emms is busy." Since the Squire's death Emms had combined with her own work that of being lady's maid to Ellen and her sister.

"Well, I don't suppose I would have remembered her then if she is only a housemaid," said Mrs. Julius, smiling. "One never does notice housemaids much, does one? I mean, one hears them sweeping and so on in one's dressing-room but they are negligible people, really."

"They wouldn't be so negligible if they weren't there," observed Josey drily.

"Oh, but, Josey, one could not imagine life without housemaids!" cried Mrs. Julius, shocked. She had very little sense of humor and took everything literally, and Josey could seldom resist teasing her. "Who would dust the rooms and do the fires and take hot water round to the bedrooms?" She smiled at the two little girls. "Well, my pets, take your fingers out of your mouths and give me another kiss and tell me what you have been doing today."

The children kissed her obediently, being careful not to touch her dress, and then their fingers went back into their mouths as they tried to think of something to say. Polly's departure on top of Nurse's admonitions had set a gulf between them and their pretty mother that, small as they were, they could not bridge.

"Would you like to look at the Chinese cabinet again?" asked Josey, coming to the rescue, and they assented eagerly, the fingers coming out with a pop.

"It's their evening treat," she told her cousin's wife. "We take everything out and put it back again. . . ."

"Don't let them spoil anything," said Mrs. Julius, who had much the same idea as Lady Augusta where the behavior of children was concerned.

"Oh dear, no," said Josey carelessly. "They are very careful little creatures, these daughters of yours, Marian!"

The Chinese cabinet was small and made of black lacquer, inlaid with mother of pearl. There were pictures on the doors in different colored lacquer of mountains and clouds and a little house where a tiny man with a beard looked out of a Chinese heaven. The doors opened to reveal small drawers, each with an ivory handle, and when they were pulled open all sorts of treasures were there to be examined: watch-guards, ivory fish, a few old samplers, counters, a box of spillikins, quill pens with worked-silk tassels, old coins, and a Chinese lady's shoe, too small even to fit Baby Julius. The children forgot their shyness of their mother as they brought the things for her to see and admire before putting them back again, the samplers carefully folded, the ivory fish in their little ivory box. The allotted hour flew by and they were scarcely ready for Polly when she came for them.

They went at once, however, without argument, only wanting to have everything out of the cabinet again so that Polly could see the treasures too.

"Some other day," she said, smiling, as their hands clasped hers. "Some other day, my darlings. . . ."

Mrs. Julius watched them go with relief mingled a little with regret. It was so easy for strangers to gain her children's affection, but she supposed that was one of the penalties for having nurses for one's children, and she could no more imagine her nursery without nurses in it than she could see the Manor without housemaids. One hour of the little girls' company exhausted her, while as for Baby Julius, every time he choked when she was holding him, he frightened her to death. . . .

The days passed so quietly and so happily that Polly scarcely noticed their passing. One day melted into the next, as the clouds at sunset melted into the violet of the night. And during the afternoons, when she walked with the children down in the woods, more often than not they would meet Mr. Charles, and he would stop and speak to the children and smile at her and exchange a few words with her before going on his way.

His presence in the woods became part of the magic of those days, of that wonderful, carefree summer, until, like the Beast in the fairy tale, Lady Augusta came home and tore it all apart.

The first intimation that Polly had was when Nurse was

sent for one evening after the children were in bed, and returned to the nursery very red in the face, very angry and out of breath, what with her stoutness and the steepness of the back stairs.

"Polly," she said at once, "whatever have you been doing in the afternoon? You tell me the truth, my girl, and don't you dare to tell me any lies!"

Polly dropped the little dress she was smocking as if it had burnt her fingers, while she crimsoned with astonishment.

"What do you mean, Nurse Crampton?" she asked. "What should I have been doing beyond taking the little girls for a walk?"

"That's just what I want to know," said Nurse ominously, and then Polly thought she knew what had happened.

"It's James that's been making mischief, I suppose," she said resentfully. "I thought he would, directly I saw him there today—"

"James?" Nurse looked surprised. "Certainly not! James has had nothing to do with it." She saw Polly bite her lip and she went on slowly, "Her ladyship's been asking questions of Miss Susan and Miss Miriam and they said as you read to them fairy stories down in the woods, instead of taking them for walks. . . ."

Polly raised her head quickly. "But only when they get too hot, Nurse Crampton! You know how they race and tear about down there. I take the book of fairy tales with me so that I can make them sit still a little while and cool off. You know that, because I asked you, and you said it was a good idea, now didn't you? There's nothing wrong in it, surely?"

"No," said Nurse thoughtfully. "Nothing ... but it seems that young Mr. Charles goes that way too and has met you and the children there more than once. . . ."

Polly found herself blushing.

"Why yes, he does take the short cut through to the Common sometimes," she said unwillingly. "But then lots of people do ... her ladyship couldn't mind that, could she? And how would it affect me?" Her eyes met Nurse

Crampton's guilelessly, and then her blush deepened while her heart seemed to stop for a moment at the meaning she saw there. "Oh, but surely her ladyship couldn't think that I take the children that way because—" She broke off, unable to put the very idea of such a suspicion into words.

"From what I know of her ladyship," said Nurse grimly, "she could think almost anything she had a mind to think, and there's nothing to stop her." She sat down heavily on the other side of the nursery table. "Polly, my dear, you must be careful not to set people talking, otherwise you'll lose your character as sure as my name's what it is. Especially if you go talking too freely to young gentlemen like Mr. Charles."

Polly was thankful that Lady Augusta had not heard about her tea with Mr. Charles in the Broughton Market tea-shop. Innocent as it had been, she felt that her character would have been in shreds after such an episode.

"But, Nurse Crampton," she protested feebly, "Mr. Charles is a clergyman. . . ."

"He could be a bishop, Polly, and it would make no difference. You are a pretty girl, and he is a young gentleman with a young gentleman's instincts, and some of them rather odd ones if you can believe all you hear. So just you take care, and if you follow my advice you'll walk with the little girls where you can be seen from the house, and you'll avoid the woods in future."

Another protest rose to Polly's lips, to be regretfully stifled. "Very well, Nurse," she said meekly, and she took up the smocking again and thought of the woods with a sigh of rebellious longing.

The way the sunlight came through the trees, the smell of the young bracken and the tufts of thyme, the quietness of it all, broken only by the cooing of the wood pigeons and the distant cawing of the rooks across the park, it had all been a perfect setting for the book of fairy tales, the pages turned eagerly by two pairs of small, hot hands.

It had needed a mind like Lady Augusta's to spoil beauty such as that, it had needed a hand as heavy as hers to crush the sunlight out of life. . . . Polly would not admit even to herself that she had waited recently for the sound of a firm footstep on that mossy path, and that she had listened for a gay voice bidding them good day, that she might have watched for a pair of eyes that would hold hers a moment before their owner smiled at her. Because that was a fairy tale too, that had become pure fantasy, a make-believe that had no real part in her life, a dream that held the magic of the Brothers Grimm, a story that only children would believe in. ... The Prince and the Goosegirl ... who was herself a goose. ... A Cinderella without a Fairy Godmother ... and with only a pumpkin for a head.

She sighed again, and laid aside the little dress and went off to bed.

But as she brushed out her hair she did not doubt in her mind that Nurse was right. It was as well to give up such dreaming while there was time, and in future she would take the children into the park and sit with them under an oak tree when they got tired, in full view of the Manor windows. And if she should see Mr. Charles Harroby approaching, she thought defiantly, she would pick them up, one under each arm, and she would run like mad, and she hoped that her ladyship would see her.

But though she tried to laugh about it her heart felt sore, and that night, as she twisted and turned on the bed in Agnes's room, she tried to conjure up the thoughts she used to have about silver trays and hot-house peaches and champagne, and ladies' maids with footmen behind their chairs. Somehow such visions would no longer come, however tightly she shut her eyes against the moonlight that crept across the floor. She kept on seeing, in the midst of it all, a pair of quizzical gray eyes, looking at her as if she puzzled their owner not a little, and she kept hearing his voice saying: "Good afternoon, Polly! How are you to-day?"

Not a cool: "Good afternoon, Nurse. How are the children today?" but a warm, human, interested, "How are *you* today?"

How are you, Polly, with your corn-colored hair and your pretty tanned face? How are you in your stiff white dress that cannot hide your graceful young figure? How are you with your shy, tell-tale eyes and your capable young hands, holding fast to the children? . . . Are you thinking things that should not be there at the back of your mind? Are you dreaming dreams above your station, in your little room on the nursery floor at the Manor, under its gabled roof?

Only this afternoon Charles had stopped again, and this time he had sat down on the same fallen tree-trunk beside her, telling her to go on reading, and as she read she had been conscious of his eyes on her face, and the smile at the corner of his mouth as he listened.

Neither heard James until he was almost upon them, taking the path through to the Common. As his shadow fell across them Polly had looked up with a start, and seeing who it was she had crimsoned with a feeling of guilt for which she could not account. What was James to her, after all, that she should feel guilty as if he had caught her out in something shameful, instead of just reading from a book of fairy tales to the children and their cousin?

But her voice had faltered and stopped and she had smiled at James and seen no answering smile on his face.

His eyes, meeting hers for a second, had passed on at once to her companion, who had given him the careless salutation that he usually gave to the men on his cousin's estate.

" 'Afternoon, James!" he said.

"Good afternoon, sir," James replied, touching his cap, but he was frowning as he walked on down the path.

"If he'd only stopped and said something," mourned Polly. "If it was no more than that it was a nice day . . . I wouldn't feel so bad about it. But he looked at me as if I was a stranger . . . and I wasn't doing anything wrong. He could have stayed and listened to the old fairy tales too if he wanted. . . . Mr. Charles wouldn't have minded."

But she knew in her heart that Mr. Charles *would* have minded, and that he would have thought it a piece of confounded cheek on James's part. For all his talk of equality when he was in the pulpit he was still a Harroby and he had inherited the Harroby pride.

And so the wretched feeling of guilt remained with her, laying heavy on her heart, and she was glad when Nurse was invited to take supper with Mrs. Grim in the housekeeper's room the next Sunday night, so that she would have to sit upstairs with the children in her absence, instead of going out. Polly did not mind forgoing her Sunday evening off: she did not in the least wish for a walk through the scented country lanes with a silent, frowning James. . . .

A bat squeaked outside her window, an owl hooted mournfully across the park, to be answered by a shrill tu-whit from another, and, with her hair gleaming gold over the pillow, uneasily Polly Kettle slept. . . .

12

THE wedding invitations arrived in their neat cardboard
boxes, and Ellen and Josey helped their mother to write
them. Emily Harrison also came up from the Rectory in
the afternoons to give a hand, because there were a great
many to send out and writing the envelopes alone needed
all the time she could give. Emily was proud of her hand-
writing: it was flowing but neat, it had character but it
was nicely legible, it showed no effort, and she liked to
think that it was the neat, educated hand of a lady.

The wedding, fixed now for the end of July, was still
six weeks away when the final envelope was written, the
final bunch of invitations put out for the post. The caterers came from London for a preliminary survey, consulting the head gardener, Graves, where it was best to have
the marquees; and the red carpet and the awning from the
church porch to the lychgate was unearthed and taken out
and beaten on the green, under the summer sun. A Hun-
garian band had been engaged, and the white satin wedding-dress was almost finished, while London was being
searched for the promise of orange blossom.

The decorations in the church were to be left to the
Manor gardeners, who, under Graves, were also to make
the bouquets, Ellen's to be of white hot-house roses from
the Manor, with myrtle in it from the bush that had been
grown from a sprig in her mother's wedding bouquet forty
years ago. New uniforms were ordered for the servants,
and an army of old retainers, pensioned off and living in
cottages and almshouses on the estate, were brought in to
give their mite of polishing and burnishing and dusting of
rooms, furniture, and plate, for Miss Harroby's wedding.

Mrs. Grim and Cook went nearly mad with the orders

that were issued from Lady Augusta's little morning-room, and then countermanded and given again, and the lists of guests were changed from day to day as various members of the family were boarded out at the Windovers' and at Lady Gregson's, and at many of the other big houses round about.

It was small wonder that the prospective bridegroom fled from all these fevered preparations and made such fleeting visits to the Manor that nobody seemed to know or care if he were there or not. Certainly nobody had any time to entertain him, except during the evenings when Josey played duets with her sister, and he was required to sing. He had a baritone voice of which he was rather proud, and when the notes of Tosti's "Goodbye" rang out through the rooms, with its thunderous piano accompaniment, Lady Augusta felt bound to admit that Ellen might have done worse.

She was happily ignorant of the Major's activities during the afternoon when Ellen was busy unpacking wedding-presents, which were beginning to arrive by the van-load, and making lists of the givers of epergnes and entrée dishes. But Polly could have told her exactly what the Major had been up to, out of sight of Lady Augusta and her daughters, and she began to wonder which might be the greater of the two evils: to be accused of laying in wait for Mr. Charles in the woods, or being forced to watch for the Major every afternoon, so that she could escape him before he caught sight of her.

"Polly, my dear," Nurse Crampton began one evening over the nursery mending, after the children were in bed.

"I know what you are going to say, Nurse," said Polly in an aggrieved voice. "And you need not say it. I *do* take care not to come anywhere near the Major if I can help it. But he's got such nasty, sneaking ways, always creeping round behind me in the park, and lurking round corners in the passages, and trying to kiss me behind cupboard doors. . . . It's as much as I can do not to slap his face—I'm sure I will one day! And he smells of that horrible brandy he keeps in his room. How Miss Ellen will ever put up with him is beyond me!"

"She'll have to put up with more than the smell of brandy if she marries him!" retorted Nurse Crampton grimly.

"*If* she marries him?" repeated Polly, wide-eyed. "Why, of course she'll marry him, Nurse. Look at all those wedding-presents downstairs—she'll never be able to send all them back! And the wedding-dress coming tomorrow by special train. . . ."

"There's many a slip!" Nurse Crampton pursed her lips. "I wouldn't put anything past that Major, though don't you say as I said so! If there was a wife and a trail of children waiting at the church door on the wedding-day it wouldn't surprise me in the least, and I'm not the only one that thinks so. I remember a very handsome groom of the chambers once, in one of the houses I was in when I was young—nobody every dreamed he was married until—" She broke off.

"Until what?" asked Polly breathlessly.

"Never you mind," said Nurse irritatingly. "It's not a story fit for your young ears."

A lamp was burning on the table between them, its golden circle clear-cut on the green serge tablecloth, and a moth came fluttering against the hot glass globe and fell, a casualty with feebly beating wings, in that warm circle.

"Nurse Crampton," said Polly slowly, "I've often wondered, how do you *know* if a man is really in love with you?"

Nurse looked at her shrewdly.

"I suppose by the way he looks at you, my dear." Her sharp voice had lost its edge and it was more gentle than Polly had known it. But did she mean, by that, the way Mr. Charles looked, Polly wondered—sort of amused and dismayed and admiring all at once? Or did she mean the way James looked, grave and kind and tender? . . .

"And the tone of his voice as he speaks to you," Nurse went on. "Gentle and humble, as if he thought you were too good for him by far. . . ."

But that *was* James, of course . . . or at least it had been James, until that unlucky afternoon down in the woods. Now he never came near her, and if she went into the stable yard he took no notice of her at all.

"And it's the way he wants you, and no other, to share his life with him," said Nurse.

"You . . . and no other . . ." echoed Polly bleakly. She tried to see Nurse's expression on the other side of the table but her face was in shadow beyond the glow of the lamp. "Did you . . . were you ever loved like that?" she asked.

There was something about little Polly Kettle that disarmed you, Nurse Crampton thought, biting off her thread sharply. If it had been Agnes sitting there asking such questions she would have shut her up pretty quick, but this girl was different. There was a warmth and sympathy about her that opened your heart to her and made you forget the bitterness that had encased you in starch and wisdom beyond your years from the time you were twenty.

"Well," she said slowly, her voice not quite steady, "there was a young man once, when I was about your age, Polly. He was called Ben—his mother named him Benjamin because he was the youngest of the family—he came courting me for three years before his regiment was sent out to the Crimea. . . ." She paused and another moth, undeterred by his predecessor's corpse that lay there on the table, came and beat his wings too against the lamp-glass before dropping down beside it.

"He didn't come back," said Nurse and her voice hardened, grating a little. "There's people that will tell you that the scum of the earth go into the Army, but don't you believe it. There's others as will tell you that if they die fighting it's only what they deserve and what they want . . . but don't you believe that, either. Wars is wicked, cruel things, Polly my dear, never intended by God, and they take the brightest and the best . . . the very best . . . like my poor Ben."

Polly sat very still, her needle poised over a little white sock, her face soft with compassion. She wanted to say something that would comfort the woman on the other side of the nursery table, but everything she thought of sounded impertinent, and while she hesitated the moment was lost.

"If that's Miss Susan's sock you're mending," Nurse Crampton said briskly, "you'd best let me see how you are doing it before you go on. I don't want to see a thread out of place, and if it isn't done to my liking I shall unpick it and you will have to do it again. . . ."

Polly laughed and surrendered the little sock to her obediently. "I don't mind, Nurse dear," she said. "It's good of you to teach me and I'll be glad to learn, though I shall never be able to do the neat mending and the lovely needlework that comes so naturally to you." She got up. "I'm going to shut that window and stop the moths coming in. They do nothing but burn themselves up against the lamp-glass, silly things. . . ."

But she remembered Nurse Crampton's warning and she avoided the Major more than ever, although as time went on and he took up his permanent abode at the Manor it became increasingly difficult. There seemed to be no end to the impudence of the man: he would make any excuse to stop and talk to the children, and even if Miss Ellen were with him he would appraise their pretty nursemaid with his bold eyes until it was obvious that Miss Harroby noticed it. There was an edge now in her voice on the rare occasions when she spoke to Polly, and the girl longed sometimes for the old security of the servants' hall where the exasperating Major would not dare to pursue her.

True he did not reach the nursery, being afraid of Nurse Crampton's gimlet eyes, but when Polly took the little girls for their afternoon walks she had to try a new direction nearly every day to avoid the advances of the amorous gentleman. She felt that nobody could be as relieved as herself when the wedding was over and the Major and his bride safely gone from the Manor.

Agnes was to come back on the day after the wedding.

"After your nice little Polly," Mrs. Julius said to Lady Augusta, "I shall be quite sorry to see that flighty nurse-

maid of mine back again. Polly is such a good, steady girl,
and so excellent with the children, Nurse Crampton says."

"Why do you have Agnes back again, then?" Lady Augusta was always eager to give away her servants, holding
that nobody could have better-trained ones than there
were at the Manor. "You are welcome to take Polly with
you when you go, dear. I am sure Mrs. Grim could spare
her to you quite easily."

Mrs. Julius shook her head.

"Oh no!" she said with a little laugh. "I couldn't rob
Mrs. Grim of Polly! Nor could I consider her as a nursemaid. She's much too pretty!"

Lady Augusta was shocked. "You don't mean ...
Julius?" she hazarded.

"Julius? Certainly not!" Mrs. Julius was indignant, and
her aunt apologized for her unworthy suspicions. She went
on more calmly: "It is the barracks that I have in mind,
Aunt Augusta! All the soldiers for miles around would be
after the girl. My back door would never be free of
them."

Lady Augusta said no more, but she privately agreed
with her nephew's wife that a maid as pretty as Polly
might be a liability. She would wait until after the wedding when Agnes was back, and then she would have a
word with Mrs. Grim about her. Lady Gregson had been
complaining lately of the difficulty in finding a nice girl as
lady's maid. Little Polly was quick and neat-fingered: she
was good at dressing hair, and Nurse Crampton was loud
in her praise of her skill with a needle. . . . Polly might be
just the sort of girl that Lady Gregson was looking for. . . .

The days went by, slowly for some, too quickly for others, and it was now the last Tuesday in July, the wedding
being fixed for the Thursday of that week.

Ever since Sunday the Major had been exhibiting a
strange restlessness: he appeared to wish to avoid his fiancée, and only Lady Augusta's firmness prevented him
from evading the garden party that the Windovers were
giving for him and Ellen on Tuesday afternoon.

In a corner of the marquee after tea, Charles came
upon him imbibing champagne in large quantities, al-

though it would seem from his glassy eyes that he had had enough already.

"Charles!" He caught at young Harroby's coat-sleeve with despairing hands. "Get me away from this place, will you? I can't meet any more of these awful people. I thought Crabb was going to be here, but I might have known he wouldn't face it."

Charles glanced from his ashy face to the crowded lawns, where Lady Augusta's black toque—she had put off her widow's weeds for the week of the wedding—was accompanied by the flower-trimmed straw of Ellen, not very far away.

He put his hand under the bridegroom's arm and conducted him swiftly out of the back of the tent, where, among a shambles of dirty wineglasses and teacups, they were conveniently hidden by a canvas screen.

"What is the matter?" asked Charles unsympathetically. "Too much champagne?"

Archie Goodyer shook his head wanly.

"No, my dear chap," he said thickly. "Too much Ellen ... *far* too much Ellen! ... I told her I didn't want to come, but she said Crabb would be here, and her mother wished it. ... But I'm going now. Get me away from this crowd, Charles, without anyone seeing me, and I'll be your friend for life."

Charles melted a little. He could well believe that the Major might be feeling satiated with Ellen's dictatorial ways, which had been becoming more autocratic as the days went by. It was the wedding, he thought, that had gone to her head.

"I'll drive you home in the Rectory gig if you like," he said shortly. "And I'll ask Emily to beg a lift home from Cousin Augusta. I'll tell her that you are not feeling well."

"Bless you, dear chap ... you're a Christian." The Major waited, looking very green, while Charles went to find Mrs. Harrison. He did not succeed, but he came upon Josey being entertained by Sir John Gregson, who was the world's greatest bore, and he wondered why it was that Josey allowed herself to attract the bores of any entertainment she happened to attend, and thought that perhaps it was due to her kindness of heart, because nobody else had time for them. He drew her a little aside and told her about the Major and she promised to collect Emily and bring her home with them.

"Poor Archie!" she said with a wicked little twinkle, before turning back to the waiting Sir John. "It was mean of Ellen to tell him that Crabb would be here. She knows as well as I do that wild horses wouldn't drag him to anything of this sort!" As he went off to find Archie, Charles heard her say: "I'm so sorry, Sir John, that we were interrupted ... I was so interested in what you were saying about that salmon you caught last year. I *do* hope you had it stuffed. ..."

Charles drove the bridegroom to the Rectory and made him lie flat on the sofa in old Lionel's study for a time, while he brought him soda-water to drink, and after a while the invalid recovered. He lost his glassy stare and the color came back to his pallid face.

"Lucky chap," he groaned, watching Charles as he took up some correspondence that had come by the afternoon's post. "Still as free as air. Sometimes, when I look back on that night, I think I must have been out of my mind."

"What night?" asked Charles, slitting the envelopes of his letters neatly with a paper-knife.

"The night that I asked Ellen to marry me," said the Major. "It was the debts that did it ... and the thought of all that money lying idle ... and then Crabb said—" He broke off.

"I wouldn't pay much attention to what Crabb says, if I were you," said Charles. "He talks too much, and most of it's nonsense."

"I know. These last few weeks have been an eye-opener to me, Charles. I can see now who is going to wear the trousers in my future ménage, and I'm beginning to wonder if seventy thousand pounds is worth it. It is all very well for Ellen to boast about gaining her independence on the day she marries, but what about me? From the way she's been arranging to rent the house and furniture, and fixing up our honeymoon trip without consulting me, it looks as if my independence is to be sunk for ever, and I don't like it. A chap has got a bit of pride, after all, and even Giles looks at me with contempt these days. . . . If I saw a chance I'd get out of it now, while there is time!"

"Get out of what? Your wedding? Oh, but that's absurd!" Charles was lightly amused. "You are suffering from pre-wedding nerves, my dear fellow. I've heard that it attacks bride and groom on these occasions, and I dare say that is why Ellen is appearing rather more . . . autocratic . . . these days. She's just as nervous as you are under the surface."

"She hides it very well then, that's all I can say." The Major put his head in his hands. "Do you know what happened yesterday afternoon? I had just stopped a moment to say good afternoon to that pretty little nursemaid of Mrs. Julius's—I swear that was all I said! Well, I might have said she was looking charming, or something of the sort. You know how it is!"

"I'm afraid I don't," said Charles stiffly. He put down his letters and the laughter left his face.

"There's no need to be priggish about it, even if you are a parson. I tell you, it was a perfectly innocent conversation that I was having with the girl, and I heard a sound behind me and there was Ellen, glaring at me as if she'd caught me at the jam. She was quite rude to the poor girl, too. 'I thought you were supposed to be taking the children for a walk?' she said, and she whisked me off to make more lists of wedding-presents. I never wish to see another cruet in my life!" He rambled on, but Charles lost interest. He laid aside his letters and said that he had to go out.

"You are welcome to the sofa as long as you care to stay," he added. "I dare say Cousin Augusta and the girls won't be back till seven."

"The girls!" The Major laughed hollowly. "Now if it were little Polly I was going off with on Thursday it would be a very different matter. One could dispense with ceremony, and if the dear little creature was ignorant of the ways of this wicked world, what a pleasure it would be to teach her! You ought to have a look at her the next time you are at the Manor and the children are about. That hair of hers, and that complexion, and those large blue eyes! ... Even if you are a parson I'll bet you'd notice them!"

Feeling that if he stayed another moment he would be forced to clout the Major with old Lionel's paperweight, Charles left him to his sofa and hurried away to the green, where the village cricket eleven were waiting to be coached in bowling.

He was sorry afterwards that he did not stay to see Archie back to the Manor. Yet how could he have guessed that he would not return there when he left the Rectory? And having returned himself later and found his visitor gone, how was he to guess, in heaven's name, where he had gone and what he was doing?

13

LADY Augusta returned with her daughters punctually at seven o'clock, but before she started to dress for dinner Ellen sent Emms to find Giles and enquire from him how his master was.

The woman came back to say that Giles had taken advantage of the Major's absence to go out that afternoon and had not yet returned, and Ellen frowned, thinking that after next Thursday Master Giles must be taught to mend his ways. In the meantime she sent for Albert and told him to go to the Major's room and find out how he was feeling, and in a few minutes the footman returned to say that the Major was not in his room and that it did not look as if he had been there either.

"The gentleman's clothes are laid out ready in his dressing-room, Miss Ellen," he said. "I expect Giles did that before he went out."

"Very considerate of him!" said Ellen angrily, tapping her foot impatiently and thinking of Giles's impending dismissal with relish. She never allowed the slightest liberties where servants were concerned, and had no patience with Josey, who would chatter to the rawest kitchen-maid as if she were a personal friend.

"I expect the Major is still at the Rectory, my dear," said Lady Augusta soothingly. "No doubt Charles is keeping him there until he feels better." She dispatched a note at once to the Rectory telling Charles to come up to the Manor for dinner at eight, and to bring Mrs. Harrison and the Major with him.

But when eight o'clock came Charles and Mrs. Harrison entered the drawing-room alone.

"I'm sorry, Augusta," Emily said. "We could not bring

Archie with us, because he is no longer at the Rectory. Charles left him in the study when he went to coach the cricket eleven on the green, and as he had gone when he got back he concluded that he must have felt well enough to come back here."

"He did not come back here!" said Lady Augusta sharply, and then she added more uncertainly, "At least, I don't think he did." She went on after a barely perceptible pause: "Do you know, I have forgotten to say good night to the pets in the nursery? Nurse Crampton will never forgive me if I omit such an important duty! If you will excuse me, Emily, I will go up and see them at once, before we sit down to dinner."

"Don't trouble yourself, Aunt Augusta!" said little Mrs. Julius. "You must be tired after your long afternoon, and I am sure Nurse won't mind."

"It is no trouble," said her husband's aunt graciously. "And I am never tired, my dear!" Such weakness she left to lesser women, and as she turned towards the door Ellen followed her.

"I will come with you, Mater," she said firmly, and they went up to the nurseries together.

The children were in bed, and Nurse Crampton had gone down to have a comfortable gossip in Mrs. Grim's room before her own supper was brought upstairs. Polly was in the nursery alone, sitting in the window and catching the last of the daylight for her sewing, but she put it down and got to her feet quickly as Lady Augusta came into the room.

Her ladyship seemed disappointed to hear that the children were already asleep, and begged her not to disturb them on any account, but Ellen walked round the room, carefully examining the children's toys, and looking behind the nursery screen, and even inside the tall toy-cupboard, as if she were expecting to find somebody lurking there.

"We are a little worried about Major Goodyer, Polly," said her ladyship at last, after she had admired the embroidery that the girl was doing on Susan's dress. "He did not feel well, and we thought he came home early from Lady Windover's, but he does not appear to be here."

"Oh," said Polly innocently, "yes, he did come back, my lady. We saw him from the nursery window while the children were sitting having their supper. He was riding one of the horses down the avenue ... the big black horse. I think he is called Emperor."

"Of course!" Lady Augusta's eyes met her daughter's again across the shadowy room. "He said he might be taking a ride this evening to see some friends ... we had forgotten that. No doubt he felt well enough to go, after all. But we must go down now, or we shall be keeping dinner waiting." She nodded graciously to the slender figure in the window. "If your sewing improves as it has done over the past few weeks," she said kindly, "I shall tell Mrs. Grim to recommend you to Lady Gregson, if she has not found a lady's maid by the time Agnes comes back. You will not want to go back to housemaid's work, I am sure, if you can sew as finely as that! ... Good night, Polly!"

Polly said, "Good night, m'lady ... good night, Miss Ellen," in a bewildered little voice, and sat down again to her sewing, but it was getting too dark to see now without a lamp, and instead of lighting it she sat on for a time staring out at the park and the avenue and the shadows that were taking the trees into their keeping on that summer evening.

A few weeks ago the suggestion that she should be recommended for a position as lady's maid—even to old Lady Gregson—would have filled her with delight, because it would have been a big step forward along the dazzling road that led to the silver breakfast-trays and the champagne and the hothouse peaches. But now she felt only dismay and apprehension, as if she might be packed off in disgrace because she had done something that made her no longer welcome at the Manor.

But though she searched the corners of her conscience she could find nothing in it to upbraid her, and she was still worrying about it when Nurse returned and scolded her for sitting there idle in the dark, and not making use of the hands that God had given her.

Downstairs dinner went through all the courses of soup, fish, entrée, meat, sweet, savory, and dessert, and the ladies retired to the drawing-room, leaving Charles to a solitary glass of port. And still Major Goodyer had not returned and neither had he sent a message to allay the fears that his behavior might be causing his betrothed. By ten o'clock not only Lady Augusta but Charles and Mrs. Harrison were feeling concerned about him, while Mrs. Julius watched Ellen in vain for some sign that she too was feeling the strain. But Ellen showed no concern at all: if she were at all apprehensive it was not so much for the Major's safety as that her independence might slip through her fingers at the last moment.

To calm their nerves Josey sat down at the piano and began playing Beethoven quietly: she found the music of that composer the greatest comfort when things threatened to get out of hand. It had a very calming influence in times of mental or emotional stress.

At eleven o'clock Emily suggested timidly that she should return alone to the Rectory, leaving Charles to wait up at the Manor for the Major's return. "In case," she added, "anything should have happened, dear!"

"And what *could* have happened?" demanded Lady Augusta impatiently. "My dear Emily, have you forgotten that the wedding is only two days away?" Her tone implied that it was a very brave man indeed who would risk his neck under such circumstances, and Emily agreed with her hastily.

"I know dear Archie is a very good rider," she said, trying to soothe her sister-in-law and only making matters worse. "But Emperor *is* a bad-tempered horse, isn't he, Augusta?"

"Julius said once that he ought to have been shot," said Mrs. Julius. "Wasn't it Emperor who killed one of your men, Aunt Augusta?"

"The man was a groom," interposed Ellen coldly. "And he stupidly got in the way of Emperor's hoofs. . . . He'd been warned."

"But Pater had to pay his widow compensation, all the same," said Josey, with an impish look at her sister over the top of the piano. "Because he was just as dead as if he'd been a noble lord and killed in the hunting field."

"I'm not in the least nervous over Archie," said Ellen contemptuously. "He is not a fool, and we were told that he was *riding* Emperor—not running behind him."

Charles, however, readily offered to stay on up at the Manor, and Emily went off thankfully to the Rectory, while the ladies at the Manor retired to bed. But midnight had come and gone before there was any sign or sound of the missing bridegroom.

Mrs. Grim's dreams were already being haunted by the last-minute arrangements that still had to be made for the reception of the friends and relatives of the bride who were to descend upon the Manor like locusts later on that day, when at half past two in the morning Charles heard the sound of singing coming up the avenue.

He got up out of his chair and hurried to the front door and there he saw the figure of the Major, walking from side to side up the long avenue in the moonlight, waving his arms over his head, and only too evidently completely drunk. Of Emperor there was no sign.

Charles saw at once that if he wished to avoid rousing the household he must at once join that inebriated figure and somehow stop it from lifting its voice in song, so he ran out and met it and seized it by the arm and shook it and besought it to make less noise.

"It's nearly three o'clock, man!" he said. "You'll wake the household. . . ."

"Don't care if I do!" said the Major with a chuckle. "Less wake the damn' lot, ole chap . . . less wake the whole damn' lot. . . ." He opened his mouth and would have launched into "Alice, where art thou?" if he had not run into a laurel bush, which sobered him up a little.

"Where in heaven's name have you been?" demanded Charles fiercely. "How could you be such a damned idiot! . . ."

" 'Ush!" His companion turned round to wag a finger at him reprovingly. "Mustn't swear, my boy! Remember your cloth . . . Remember, remember, the fifth of November!" This struck him as being so humorous that he shouted with laughter, and Charles was not surprised to see a light flicker up in the menservants' wing. As he reached the entrance hall he was met by Harris and Albert, the latter holding a candle aloft, and the butler clad in a dressing-gown that had once belonged to Sir John and was a great deal too large for him.

"Oh, Mr. Charles!" he exclaimed. "Whatever has happened to the Major? Is he ill?"

"No." Charles was short and to the point. "Only drunk ... where is his man?"

Harris shook his head. "Like master, like man," he murmured. "Albert has just finished putting him to bed, and it's my belief he won't wake till midday tomorrow ... or I should say today, sir!"

"Then there's no help for it. We'll have to get him upstairs between us." Charles renewed his grip on his charge. "I don't want any of the ladies to see him in this condition, Harris. He's very drunk indeed."

"*Not* drunk!" Archie broke away from Charles's restraining hand and made a staggering dash for the stairs. "Not drunk at all ... only very unhappy ... very, very unhappy—" Here he fell flat on his face, and Charles and Albert had some difficulty in getting him on his feet again. After a short struggle they managed to get him up to the first landing, where he broke away from them again and, in fact, escaped them altogether, letting out a view-hallo as he reeled off down the corridor, his objective being the staircase that led to the nurseries.

Before he could be checked he was at the bottom of the stairs, still view-halloing at the top of his voice, and shouting for Polly in between.

Nobody could have slept through such a din, and neither Ellen nor her mother were asleep. They struggled into dressing-gowns and came out on to the corridor, where the lamps had been turned low, lighted bedroom candles in their hands, and were joined there by Josey and Marian.

The Major was by this time half-way up the stairs, and as Charles reached him he saw a door open at the top and Polly come out. She stood there for a moment in her nightdress, her candle in her trembling hand, and her golden hair streaming over her shoulders, while the two little girls clasped her round the knees, gazing down with scared eyes at the gentleman who was making all the noise.

As Charles ran up behind him Archie Goodyer made a last strenuous effort to clutch hold of Polly's feet.

"Pretty lil' Polly!" he shouted. "Pretty lil' Polly! Let me come up to your room, m'dear, and sleep with you. . . . Don't be cruel to me, my lovely lil' charmer . . . don't send me 'way. . . ."

Here Charles's hand descended firmly on his collar, and he was swiftly turned over on his back and pulled down to the corridor below, his head bumping on every stair as he went.

"Go back to bed, Polly," said Charles urgently. "And take the children with you. . . ."

Lady Augusta and Ellen were waiting in silence, Mrs. Julius was as wide-eyed as her children, and Josey's face was brimming with laughter that she did her best to hide by clapping a hand over her mouth.

"He's ill," said Marian consolingly. "It was so hot this afternoon . . . a touch of the sun. . . ."

"A touch of the sun!" Lady Augusta conveyed the scorn of centuries of Fanes into the words. "He's *drunk*, Marian!" She turned majestically to the butler. "Harris, you and Albert had better get him into bed, and when you leave him you will kindly turn the key in the door."

"Yes, m'lady."

"Thank you, Harris. That will be all." And Lady Augusta swept back into her room without a glance at her elder daughter.

Ellen said nothing at all. She studied the Major calmly and dispassionately for a moment, and then, still in complete silence, she too walked off down the corridor and back to her own room.

The Major, after staring glassily at them all from his seat on the bottom stair, now passed out completely, and Albert and old Harris between them got him off to bed, while Charles let himself out of the house.

The dawn of a warm summer day was breaking as he made his way back across the park in the first light of the morning, and although he had never liked his cousin Ellen, he couldn't help feeling sorry for her as he went. A drunkard for a husband was no joke, and more especially if he happened to be as unscrupulous as the Major promised to be.

From Ellen and the Major his thoughts went on to Polly, standing like a guardian angel at the top of the nursery stairs. With her white night-gown hanging round her in voluminous folds, and the candlelight on her hair and the two little children clinging to her skirts, she might have been a picture painted by Burne-Jones or Rossetti or Millais. What would they have called such a picture? he wondered. "The Blessed Damozel," perhaps. . . .

The birds were singing in a chorus now to greet the dawn, the grass was wet with dew, the air as fresh as only the early morning can be after the close air of shut windows at night.

He turned aside to the woods where he could be sure of solitude, and he found the fallen log where Polly had sat and read to the children, and he sat down on it himself, his hands lightly clasped in front of him.

Across his mind the lines of Rossetti's poem came back to torment him, just eluding him, and yet clear as a mirror. The first verse was always easy to remember, and somehow it described Polly exactly as she had been, standing there at the top of the stairs. Her eyes were indeed blue and grave and deep as water, with something of its stillness in their depths.

But how did the thing go on? Blest if he could recall it. . . . There was something about her hair "lying down her back" and "yellow like ripe corn". . . . Oh, yes, and that bit about 'she scarce had been a day one of God's choristers: the wonder was not yet quite gone from that still look of hers'. . . . Polly indeed had that wondering look in her eyes . . . you might call it innocence and not be far wrong. . . .

Why did she haunt him so, this little country nursemaid? As Anna had scornfully pointed out, no doubt she had a score of rustic swains waiting to keep her company.

She had the soft speech of the country girl, and she dropped an aitch from time to time. Polly was no lady . . . but he could not get her out of his mind, his Blessed Damozel, and he wished with all his heart that he could. Because if he were to fall seriously in love with her it would not only ruin her life, but it might ruin his as well. People were not likely to trouble their heads much about young parsons who married housemaids. . . .

Married . . . here his thoughts halted again, and a feeling of dismay and delight swept over him.

To marry Polly. . . . Was he mad to think of it? Or only suddenly and completely sane?

He took out his watch and saw that it was nearly six o'clock, and he made his way back to the Rectory and let himself in by the side door and shaved and bathed and changed before going across to the church to take the service there.

He was surprised to find Josey in the Manor pew, because Lady Augusta considered it to be rather High Church to go to church on a week-day, and her daughters had been brought up in the same tradition.

After the short service he joined Josey in the porch and she explained her presence there with her impish smile.

"I felt I had to put up a quiet prayer for Ellen before the hordes of relations descend on us today. Did you manage to get dear Archie to bed all right between you? He was very drunk, wasn't he?"

"He was rather . . . I hope Ellen wasn't very upset?"

"I shouldn't think so, although I haven't seen her yet to find out, but from what I know of her present mood it will make no difference to her determination to go on with the wedding tomorrow. She is determined to marry and marry she will, even if Harris has to be there to prop up the bridegroom on one side and Albert on the other!" She added soberly, "Charles, Marian told me that Julius has not been able to find Archie's name in any army list."

"I am not surprised. Are you?"

She hesitated. "Not really, I suppose. He probably joined a Volunteer Regiment for the space of a summer,

training with them on Saturdays and Sundays when the
banks were shut."

"Do you think he was a bank clerk, then?"

"I am almost sure of it, although he has certainly
scraped up a veneer of breeding from somewhere."

"Perhaps a rich customer—a widow, you know—left
him a fortune and it went to his head."

"Or perhaps he falsified the books and won his fortune
that way."

"However he did it, he has lost it now!" He broke off
as she caught his arm and shook it, dismay in her laughing eyes.

"Charles! Do you realize that we are talking about Ellen's future husband and my future brother-in-law? And
you a parson! Aren't you ashamed?"

"Not a bit. Are you?"

"Not a scrap!" She sighed and added: "I'm sorry the
Bishop is coming to marry them. You ought to have done
it."

"What, after last night? It would have been too embarrassing for us all, my dear! The Bishop will know nothing
about Archie's little fall from grace and he will lend dignity to the occasion."

"I hope you are right. But I rather think that his lordship *will* hear of Archie's little adventure, all the same. I
have a feeling, in fact, that everybody will have heard
about it before tomorrow dawns."

"Oh, not before tomorrow, Josey. Fast as news travels
in these parts, it won't travel as fast as that!"

Again she gave him her monkeyish smile.

"I wonder if you know as much about village life as I
do, Charles? And, before I forget, Mater sent a message
when I went to say good morning to her before I came
out. We are expecting you and Aunt Emily again to dinner
tonight. Poor Mater, she looked as if she had not slept
a wink. . . . She thinks, I fancy, that it might do you good
to meet some of our more exalted relatives."

"It is very good of her to be concerned for me, but I
am sure your numbers will be sufficient without me."

"No doubt they will, but we'd like you to come, all the

same, if only to lend us moral support. You must remember that there are only two Harrobys in Holy Orders at the moment, and you are one of them, Charles. It is rather an awful thought! How shall we gain heaven with so few of our cousins there to open the gates?"

He laughed unwillingly. "Josey, you are trying to shock me, but you won't succeed. Just because I've put on a parson's collar, I have not put on with it a parson's mind."

Her fingers tightened a little on his arm. "Do you think I don't know that, Charles?"

"Bless you! I think you know me as well as I know myself, Josey . . . perhaps even better. Well then, I'll come, if only to see that the bridegroom doesn't get drunk again."

"He won't do that. We will be watching him like a covey of cats after one mouse. Poor man, he won't get away from us again before the knot is well and truly tied!"

"You are incorrigible!" He looked at the hand on his arm oddly for a moment before covering it with his and giving it a quick, cousinly squeeze. It was a firm little hand, strong and well shaped. "I can't think why you never married, Josey! Ellen I can understand . . . her coldness and self-sufficiency would repel most men. But you . . . are human!"

"And ugly," she said, taking her hand away with a laugh. "A man wants something nice to look at across the breakfast table, my dear! By candlelight, over a dinner table, it might not be so bad . . . but in the cold light of day and on an empty stomach—Brr!" She wrinkled her nose at him, and having reached the lychgate, she collected her bicycle from where it was leaning against the other side of the wall, and rode away up the path that led back to the Manor and breakfast.

14

THE first house guests at the Manor passed through the gates at noon, the last at six, and between those hours the house gradually filled to overflowing. Burke began talking darkly about the wells running dry before morning, with all the water that was being taken upstairs for baths: although the Manor wells were deep, the dry summer was leaving its mark and the water had developed a slightly brownish hue. Nurse Crampton would not allow the children to drink a drop of it unless it were boiled first, and complained that it was discoloring their white muslin dresses and cotton socks.

Excitement is infectious, and Polly's small charges were quick to catch it and get out of hand. She took them for a long walk, away from all the preparations and arrivals during the afternoon, but they could still hear the men hammering in the pegs for the big marquees on the lawn and in the park, where Lady Augusta intended to entertain the tenants of the estate and all those who worked on it on the wedding-day.

Punctually at half past six, after the last carriage-load of guests had been welcomed downstairs, Nurse sent Polly to fetch the little girls up to bed. They had been too long in the drawing-room as it was, and she knew they would be over-excited with all the admiration they were receiving.

"They'll be as cross as two sticks tomorrow," she grumbled. "If I'd had my way they wouldn't have gone down there at all tonight. I wanted them to have a quiet hour playing up here by themselves before early supper and bed. But their mother must have them downstairs to show them off to the Countess. I'm sure their grandmother would rather see them holding up their cousin's train properly tomorrow than being fractious tonight because they are over-tired. You go and fetch them now, Polly, my dear, and don't take no for an answer. Just be firm with them and say that I sent you."

So down Polly went to the white drawing-room, a large apartment running half the length of the Manor and looking out on to the terrace, and she had a little difficulty in finding the children at first, the room was so crowded and so large. When she did catch sight of them she could see at once that they were quite beyond themselves.

In front of all these guests nursery authority stood a very poor chance, unless Nurse Crampton had been there in person, and even Lady Augusta was too occupied with her guests to call them to order.

They had romped with new uncles and aunts and cousins, they had been embraced by lovely ladies, they had been smiled at and indulged with sweet cakes and chocolate biscuits and raspberries-and-cream, and they were not at all anxious to go to bed. They knew that they were being a success, and they were loath to leave the stage where they were receiving so much unaccustomed adulation, and directly they saw Polly they ran away from her, so that she had to run after them, and when she caught them Susan grabbed her cap and sent her hair tumbling down.

"Now, Miss Susan, that's naughty!" Polly wished that Nurse had left her with the baby and come down herself. "Do you want me to fetch Nurse Crampton to you?"

Susan shook her head, laughing, and ran off with Polly's cap, while the group of guests surrounding them realized that the children were becoming tiresome and suddenly fell silent. Susan was quickly caught by a masculine hand, and looking up and struggling to free herself she saw Major Goodyer's monocle above her.

"Now, little girl!" he said. "Enough of that ... you go back to your nurse. We've all had enough of you for today."

Susan glared at him and tried to free her hand, but he

held it tight, and suddenly she stopped wriggling and stood still.

"I know you!" she piped up shrilly. "You are our new cousin Archie. . . . *You* came up the nursery stairs in the middle of the night and asked Polly if you could sleep in her bed!"

The hand holding hers dropped it as if she had bitten it. A gasp went round their immediate circle, followed by a sudden hush over the entire room, while people craned their necks to see what was happening in the group round the children. A crimson-faced Polly ran forward and removed the small girls urgently and at speed, and if the matter had been allowed to rest there all might still have been saved.

But Ellen had heard the shrill child's voice and she had caught the quick glances in her direction, and her pride could not let it pass. She stopped the pretty nursemaid and said loudly and clearly: "That was a lie, Susan, and it's very naughty to tell lies. Isn't it, Polly?"

Polly looked this way and that and wished that the floor would open and swallow her up, and the furious Susan, tugging at her restraining hand, shouted out: "It isn't a lie! It's true, isn't it, Polly?"

And instead of making some excuse and hurrying the children away, poor Polly blurted out the first thing that came into her head: "The poor gentleman was drunk, dear . . . he didn't know what he was saying. . . ."

Her voice was louder than she had intended, and there came a second gasp and somewhere in the silence in the room somebody smothered a laugh. Quick as a flash Ellen's hand went out and caught the girl a stinging blow across the face, the rings she was wearing cutting it deep.

"You little slut!" she cried, her voice low and trembling. "How dare you! Leave the room at once!"

Polly never knew how she got herself and the children upstairs. She remembered a host of eyes that seemed to stare and stare as she went through them, and among them somewhere she caught sight of Mrs. Harrison's, gentle and pitying, and behind her Mr. Charles's face, red with anger. She thought that he took her hand as she passed and said something to her, but she did not know what it was. She only knew that when she arrived at last in the nursery both children were crying, and that the tears were running down her own face unchecked. Nurse Crampton exclaimed at the sight of her.

"Whatever have you done?" she cried. "There's a great bruise coming up on your left cheek and a cut above your eye—it's bleeding. . . . And where's your cap?"

"Susan snatched it off," said Polly, and she sank down at the table and gave way to her tears. "And to think that I ever wanted to go into service . . . where things like this can happen to a girl . . . to think I ever thought it would be the finest thing in the world. The silver trays, the champagne, the footmen behind the chairs. . . . I'd rather work in a shoe factory, earning two shillings a week. . . ."

Nurse stood frowning and puzzled and then she caught her shoulder and shook it.

"Enough of that!" she said firmly. "I don't want hysterics in my nursery! I'll fetch you some sal volatile to drink, while you get the children undressed and into bed, and then you can come back here and tell me quietly what happened, and what you did, and who gave you that bruise."

Her discipline was like a douche of cold water. Polly pulled herself together and obeyed her, swallowing the sal volatile and then getting the children into bed in silence, and trying not to give way to tears again when their small arms went round her neck in penitent hugs.

When they had had their supper and were tucked up in bed she went back to the nursery and told Nurse everything that had happened, and waited in unhappy silence for her verdict.

"Well," she said at last judicially, "it was your fault, of course, Polly. We know that."

Having learned to depend on Nurse's sense of fair play during the short time she had worked with her, Polly was both shocked and indignant.

"How *could* it be my fault?" she asked. "Major Goodyer did say that . . . it was true. . . ."

"I know," said Nurse grimly. "I heard him, though I

didn't go out on the landing in my night-gown to see what was going on."

Polly blushed. "He made such a *noise!*" she protested. "He woke the children . . . they were frightened. . . ."

"I dare say." Nurse Crampton sniffed. "All the same you shouldn't have said anything about him being drunk. That's where you were wrong, Polly. The first thing you learn in good service is never to back-answer anybody. If you do it to the upper servants they'll resent it and pay you out for it sooner or later, and if you back-answer the gentry you'll be dismissed without a character. So now you know."

"But . . ." Polly was horrified. "You don't think I shall be dismissed for . . . for what happened downstairs, Nurse Crampton? They couldn't . . . it isn't right, or fair. . . ."

"We'll have to wait and see about that, won't we?" Nurse was by no means reassuring. "And don't you start crying again, my dear! We may be short of water at the Manor but tears never helped nobody and never will."

Polly gave a little watery smile and she patted her shoulder comfortingly.

"You go off to bed," she said. "I'll bring you a drink of something hot and some liniment for that bruise later. Run along now, because there'll be a lot to do tomorrow."

Later on that night, however, as Nurse Crampton sat alone in the nursery, Mrs. Grim came to visit her there, with an expression of anger in her small eyes that boded ill for somebody.

"Well, Nurse!" she said in a low voice, shutting the door behind her. "I suppose you will have heard what happened downstairs before dinner?"

"Polly told me." Nurse was uncompromising and equally unsmiling. "And I may as well tell you at once, Mrs. Grim, that I cannot understand how a lady like Miss Ellen could stoop to such behavior. I've never known anything like it, not in any family that was of any standing whatever. And as for the Fanes, they are far too dignified to strike a servant—and in front of all those guests! . . . No doubt Polly was foolish, on account of her being so young, but my sympathies are entirely with her, Mrs. Grim."

"And you aren't the only one, Nurse." Mrs. Grim sniffed. "I've just had Mrs. Harrison to see me. She says that Mr. Charles wants her to offer the Rectory as ... as a refuge for Polly."

Nurse's indignation vanished before her astonishment. "A refuge?" she repeated.

"A refuge. That was the word she used." Mrs. Grim nodded, her face full of meaning. "She knows as well as you and I do, Nurse Crampton, that Polly cannot go on here at the Manor after what has happened."

"Well, no," said Nurse reluctantly. "I never thought she could ... But I can't say I ever expected *Mr. Charles* to take a hand in it!" She frowned, remembering the walks in the woods. "Polly is far too pretty," she said.

"Yes, indeed!" The housekeeper agreed with her whole-heartedly. "I've never been so deceived in anyone as I've been in Polly Kettle. Don't think she isn't a good girl, Nurse Crampton. Nobody could be better. But she was such a skinny little thing when she came to us, you could pin her through, and with that dreadful great lump of yellow hair always slipping away from its pins. ... Nobody could foresee that she would grow up so pretty! I've never chosen a girl for her looks and I never shall. The plain ones give much less trouble all round. If you have pretty maids about the place the other girls are jealous and the men can't keep their minds on their work. Polly will get into continual scrapes for her looks."

"Well, her looks aren't her fault, poor child," said Nurse stoutly. "We are as God made us, Mrs. Grim. What did you say to Mrs. Harrison?"

"I told her Polly could not be sent home in disgrace, as she had done nothing wrong," said Mrs. Grim, equally ready to defend Polly against injustice when it came to the point. "And I said that when the wedding is over tomorrow she will be free to come to her as her own personal maid. I half expected her to refuse to have her on those terms, mind you, because I don't know what that old Martha of hers will have to say when she hears about it.

She hates young maids and she is as crotchety as she is bad-tempered. But Mrs. Harrison said calmly that it would suit her very well, and if Polly packed her box to-morrow, old Herrick would come for it in the evening."

"H'm." Nurse looked annoyed. "Well, since nobody seems to have consulted *my* convenience, Mrs. Grim, I should be obliged if Polly can stay until tomorrow night, as she cannot go downstairs now with the little girls, and somebody must be here in the nursery with Master Julius while I am with them. The poor little boy has got one of his nasty colds, so that he won't be able to go out at all to-morrow, and Polly can sit with him here all day, while I take charge of Miss Susan and Miss Miriam. And if I get one naughty look from those two little madams they'll go straight back to bed, wedding or no wedding."

"I'm sure I'm very sorry, Nurse," said Mrs. Grim, trying to placate the tyrant of the nursery. "Perhaps I could find another girl to take Polly's place for the re-mainder of your stay here."

"No, thank you, Mrs. Grim!" Nurse closed her lips firmly and, after an uncomfortable silence, added thinly: "I think I've had enough of the girls here, and until Agnes comes back I will manage without a nursemaid. It isn't what I've been accustomed to, of course, but that don't matter. Her ladyship, the Countess, told me today when she came up herself to enquire after little Master Julius's cold, that they were putting his lordship's house at East-bourne at our disposal for the whole of August and Sep-tember, and I said I was very glad to hear it. There is nothing like sea air to set the children up for the winter, after all."

"Winnie could give you a hand with the washing, Nurse," said Mrs. Grim, properly impressed. "And one of the under-housemaids will clean the nurseries, and Albert can do the fires. We will do everything we can to help un-til Agnes comes back."

Nurse Crampton said nothing, but her expression said "You had better!" as loudly as any female expression could speak.

15

YET in spite of it all the wedding went off without a hitch. Everyone said afterwards how excellent it was, from the champagne at the wedding-breakfast to the elegance of the bridesmaids' dresses.

The Earl of Harrogate was there to give his cousin away, and Ellen was stately in white satin and orange blossom, and certainly looked remarkably handsome as she came down the aisle on her bridegroom's arm. The veil was thrown back from her face and her aristocratic features were made human by the flush on her cheeks, and her eyes glittered rather than shone with a light that, although it might not have been radiance, nevertheless had a satisfied look of triumphant achievement about it.

On their way back to the Manor in the open carriage Archie cleared his throat and tried to make a pretty speech.

"You are looking magnificent, my dear!" he said.

"Thank you." Her eyes were on the road, where villagers and school-children had gathered all the way to the Manor gates to cheer and wave to Lady Augusta's elder daughter, and it was not until she had been helped out of the carriage and conducted to the white drawing-room, where Edwards was waiting with the other servants to congratulate her before arranging the folds of her train around her, that she said anything more. Then she said in a tone of great satisfaction: "Mr. Pierce was there. Our eyes met as I came down the aisle and he smiled his blessing."

"Mr. Pierce?" For a moment Archie was bewildered and then he remembered a brass plate on some railings in Lincoln's Inn Fields. "Oh, ah, of course . . . the lawyer."

"Exactly! The lawyer ... he had to be here, to see that I was properly and legally married, and nobody can say now that I am not, can they? There were far too many witnesses for that! So that now, my dear Archie, I am in full possession of my godmother's fortune, and your wife is a very rich woman."

The words struck on Major Goodyer's ears with delight, and he turned impulsively to smile his appreciation and congratulations to his bride, when he met her eyes, and the look in them took the smile from his lips and the warmth from his heart. There was something here that, schemer as he was, he did not understand: it was as if a sitting partridge, plump and ready for the table, had suddenly turned itself into an eagle, far beyond his reach.

There was no time for any more, however, as Lady Augusta and Josey arrived with the Harrogates, and with them old Lord Derwentwater, who had been dragged away from his club to do the honors for Archie's relatives, conspicuous by their absence. His lordship, having been told that he was related to the Major, took no trouble to verify the information but accepted it with resignation.

"There's no knowing who one is related to these days," he complained to Crabb-Taylor. "The Derwentwaters were always notorious for their large families, on both sides of the blanket, and from the look of your cousin Ellen's young man I should say he springs from some of the less renowned members of the family."

Behind his lordship and the bridesmaids, and the two little trainbearers with the sharp-eyed Nurse Crampton, there came a stream of guests, some of them walking across the park from the church on that hot day.

Bride and groom stood side by side to receive their congratulations before they filed on into the grounds and the bride seemed to be a great deal more composed than the groom, who became more nervous and less happy under the fire of felicitations. His usual self-assurance, so much in the ascendancy of late, had disappeared, and he received the well-meant chaff from Crabb and his friends with an uneasy smile, his eyes turning frequently towards the stately bride, who never troubled to look his way.

The toasts were drunk, the three-tiered wedding-cake was cut, and the bride and groom went upstairs to change for the wedding journey.

When Ellen was ready she received Mr. Pierce in her little sitting-room with a dignity that suited her newly married state.

"You have brought my will with you?" she said. "I hope it is ready for signature."

"All ready and complete, Mrs. Goodyer." He felt himself bound, however, to utter one last protest. "You have not changed your mind about Major Goodyer? In this will, I feel I must remind you, if anything should happen to you he will not benefit by a penny."

"And why should he?" Her voice was pleasantly contemptuous. "He has served his turn by giving me my independence, and if he cares to behave himself as a gentleman should, he will be able to live comfortably for the rest of his life. I don't see that I should do more for him than provide his board and keep: it is not in the least necessary."

Accustomed as he was to the selfishness of many kinds of clients, Mr. Pierce found himself to be shocked by the lady's callous disregard for the man she had just married, but he said nothing beyond remarking coldly that in that case he would summon two of the servants to witness her signature, and the matter would be concluded.

Edwards was fetched in from the last of the packing, and Albert, who was helping Giles to take his master's luggage downstairs. Ellen signed her name boldly at the bottom of the document, the two servants witnessing it before the lawyer folded it up and returned it to his leather bag.

"You will let me have a detailed account of the money I have inherited?" said Ellen, when they were alone again. "I think you said it would come to considerably more than one hundred thousand pounds?"

"It will be quite that and more. ... It was invested in excellent shares at compound interest. You are now a wealthy woman, Mrs. Goodyer."

"I am glad to hear it." There was something a little tigerish about her smile. "And you have written to the banks at Naples and Rome?"

"Certainly. All is in order there. The papers have been sent through and you will be able to draw what amounts of money you wish when you arrive."

"Thank you. I am obliged to you. I am looking foward to seeing Italy. It is a country I have never had the opportunity of visiting before." She rose and held out her hand. "Goodbye, Mr. Pierce. I have no doubt we shall meet again sometimes when I am back in London. I have every confidence in your ability to deal with any difficulty that may arise during my absence."

He took her hand for a moment and bowed himself out, and Ellen returned to her bedroom and examined her reflection in the long cheval glass, while in the dressing-room next door Edwards packed the last of her new tortoiseshell-backed brushes in the crocodile leather travelling-case that was a wedding-present from Josey. By her side, helping her, was Nancy, who was going with Ellen to act as her maid until she could be replaced by a French-woman when they returned to England.

Country-bred, stolid as a bun, Nancy viewed the prospect in front of her with a misgiving that she was too well trained to show. Journeys to foreign parts did not attract her in the least: she had heard that the food was bad, that foreigners as a whole were excitable and incomprehensible and extremely dirty, and that their cities smelt to high heaven.

The wedding-dress had been spread out on the bed, and in front of all that symbolic grandeur of gleaming satin and lace and orange blossom, Ellen saw reflected in the glass a tall, composed woman, in a travelling dress of rose-colored cloth trimmed with black braid, her hand-some face topped by a small black toque and close-fitting veil.

A diamond brooch—her mother's gift—was pinned into the high lace neck of the dress, and a gold watch with her new initials in pearls—the gift of the bridegroom—was suspended from a pearl brooch in the shape of a lover's knot, pinned into the left side just below the lace yoke. Her gloves were of finest suede, and her black, high-heeled shoes had the toes embroidered in small black beads. She caught up a black feather-boa and put it round her shoulders, looked at herself with satisfaction, and nodded at her reflection with a slow smile.

"You will do very nicely, Mrs. Goodyer!" she murmured aloud. "Very nicely indeed!" She took up the short train to the skirt of her dress and swept to the door. "I am going now, Nancy," she said, and went on down the wide corridor to the staircase, a woman of independence and a lady of means.

It was not the best evening on which to break the news to old Martha at the Rectory that her mistress had engaged a younger maid to assist her in her work. Martha had been as interested in the wedding as anybody else in the village, she had stood about on the green outside the church until her old feet ached, and the grapevine about her, going from mouth to mouth, had been busy while they waited, so that the gossip about little Polly Kettle was relayed to her long before she heard anything about it from Mrs. Harrison. She might be forgiven, therefore, for being more short-tempered than usual.

"I didn't ask for help, did I?" she grumbled. " 'Pears to me when I do will be the time to offer it. But if you thinks as I'm too old for my work you have only to say so, ma'am, and I'll pack my box and go. I dessay there'll be a corner I can creep into in my old age. But I've worked for you and for the late Mr. Harrison for thirty years, and it's a poor reward for faithful service, and that's the Christian truth of it, ma'am." Martha never failed to speak her mind, and Emily knew it.

"Look, Martha—" she began pacifically, and was fiercely interrupted.

"There's no call to "Look Martha" me, ma'am!" said her old servant with a shake of her trembling grey head. "I knows when I'm no longer wanted, I s'pose. . . ."

"It isn't anything to do with you, Martha!" cried Emily, trying to patient. "I haven't engaged Polly because I thought you were too old for your work, or anything like it. Do you really think I'd part with you, after all the time we've been together? That's nonsense, and you must know it if you think about it at all, instead of jumping to the wrong conclusions in such a dreadful hurry! It isn't kind of you, Martha, to think such things!"

"Well, what is that young woman coming here for, then?" demanded Martha, and Emily hesitated, unable to tell the truth about the thoughts that kept her awake at night and nagged at her most of the day.

"There was a fuss up at the Manor," she said slowly. "One of those fusses that are nobody's fault . . . and innocent people get blamed for things . . . and you know what I am, Martha. I can't bear injustice, and it seemed to me to be an excellent solution for Polly to come here and give a hand with the cleaning for a time. This house is a great big barn of a place, as you have often said since we've been here, and, as the late Rector's family have been kind enough to leave Mr. Charles their furniture to use until Mr. Algy and his wife come in September, I'd like to leave it as well kept as when we found it."

"The Reverend Lionel had a staff of maids here, as well as two or three menservants," grumbled Martha. "You can't expect one pair of hands to do the work of ten."

"And I don't," cried Emily eagerly. "And that is why I thought of having Polly—to help you, Martha. She was a housemaid at the Manor until she began looking after the little girls lately, and so you will not have to teach her how to polish and dust. Doris has trained her well, I know. I'm sure you will find her a great help."

Martha was no fool and Emily guessed that she had heard quite a lot about the goings-on at the Manor but she said no more. When Polly arrived that night she conducted her to her room in frosty silence, and left her there with scarcely the civility of a good night.

It was Mrs. Harrison's habit every morning to come into the kitchen to discuss the day's meals with her old servant, and both she and Martha appreciated the ritual that accompanied these visits, from the careful dusting of the chair before she sat down, to the strange marks that Martha had made on the kitchen slate before she came, marks that meant nothing at all as there was not an item that she had forgotten, old as she was.

On the following morning, however, as Polly went upstairs to start on the bedroom work, Emily felt free to ask Martha what she thought of her new assistant.

Martha shook her head. "She's willing and pleasant enough," she said. "But she's much too pretty."

"Oh, Martha, why must you repeat what everybody else is saying?" Emily tried not to sound impatient. "The poor girl can't help her looks."

But Martha's eyes were as keen as her sense of hearing and she had observed the look on Charles's face when he had greeted Polly the night before, and she had heard the tone of his voice when he told her that he hoped she would be happy with them at the Rectory, and there was only one thought in her mind.

"As long as she knows her place and keeps to it I shall have no complaint to make," she said, folding her hands on her apron with a look of determination. "But will she, ma'am? And, what is more, will Mr. Charles let her?"

"Martha!" Emily hoped that her indignation sounded convincing. "You are not suggesting . . ."

"I'm suggesting nowt," said Martha. "Mr. Charles may be a nice young gentleman, and a Harroby, ma'am, but he's only human. He'd want to do the right thing by a girl, to my way of thinking, and the likes of you don't marry the likes of Polly, and that's the truth."

In the face of such plain speaking there seemed to be no point in trying to keep up a polite fiction any longer. Emily said feebly: "And what about Squire Benson at home? Didn't he marry his housekeeper only last year?"

"And not before it was time, as you know as well as I do, ma'am. She was six months gone when he took her to church and made an honest woman of her."

Emily made one last effort at regaining her dignity.

"I am sorry and saddened that you could think such a thing of Mr. Charles, though, Martha. He's a clergyman. . . ."

"And with some queer notions too, if you've listened to

his sermons as careful as I have, ma'am!" sniffed Martha. "He don't care much for the gentry, don't Mr. Charles. He's all for the poor creatures what is starving in the cities and being worked to death by sweated labor in the factories. ... If Polly had been a lady he would never have looked at her, however much she was put upon. But just because she's a servant he's interested in her, and it's not the thing for a young gentleman like him to do. Not brought up as he's been. ... He'd much better leave her be. It will end in disaster, you mark my words."

And this time Emily was in so much agreement with her that she had nothing to say.

Not so Lady Augusta, who arrived two days later in her carriage, demanding to see Charles. Martha showed her in, and, seeing the white-hot fury in her face, conducted her to the study in grim silence. Charles was sitting alone there, not working or writing letters, or doing anything, in fact, except staring out at the sunlit gardens with a smile on his lips.

The smile froze as her ladyship greeted him.

"Charles, this has got to stop!" she cried, scarcely waiting for the door to close before she launched her attack.

"I beg your pardon, Cousin Augusta?" One of old Lionel's gardeners was working on a flower-bed near by, and he shut the window before facing her gravely, his face more grown-up than she had ever seen it before. "I'm afraid I don't understand you."

"You understand me well enough!" She had not yet resumed her widow's weeds, and as she tossed her head the purple roses in her black straw hat quivered with her wrath. "I suppose you will not deny that it was you and you alone who forced Emily to invite my housemaid to the Rectory?"

He flushed. "I don't know what you are talking about," he said quietly. "Polly Kettle was treated shamefully by Ellen in front of a room full of your guests, and for no other reason that that she blurted out the truth about the unpleasant gentleman who is now your son-in-law. To get the poor girl out of a situation that was not her fault Cousin Emily suggested that she should come here to help old Martha. At least it will save her from being dismissed from the Manor without a character."

"As she would have been!" said Lady Augusta savagely. "Abominable little slut. . . ."

"I would be obliged if you would be more careful how you speak of Polly!" said Charles.

"What!" She could not credit herself with having heard him aright. "How dare you take that tone with me?"

"I shall take what tone I please," he replied calmly. "This is my house for the time being, and I can say what I like in it. I will not have Polly abused by you or anybody else. She has been most abominably treated by you all, in my opinion."

"And what is your opinion worth, pray? Are you trying to tell me that you have so far forgotten yourself as to develop an interest in a housemaid, Charles?"

"Well, you may say that I have, I suppose," he replied, quite unruffled. "As a matter of fact I intend to marry her, but that is entirely my business and hers."

Her face went ashy white. "Impossible!" she whispered. "Impossible!" She stared at him in horror, as the only valid reason for such a step occurred to her. "You mean that you've *got* to marry her?"

"I mean nothing of the sort." His eyes sparked fire. "If your mind is capable of understanding such a thing, I have never laid a finger on Polly, except to take her hand and bid her welcome here. But I am quite sure now that she is the sort of girl that I want for a wife . . . sweet, unselfish, unworldly. . . ."

"Enough of that!" Lady Augusta got herself up out of the chair and if he had not hated her so much he would have been sorry for her, because she looked so stricken. "I don't want to hear any more. I shall not forget this, Charles Harroby, and I shall never forgive you for bringing this disgrace upon us all. You can, in fact, marry whom you please, because from this morning I will never see you or speak to you again."

She left him standing there in old Lionel's study, defiantly unashamed, and a few days later they heard that she and Josey had travelled with Mrs. Julius and the children to the house in Eastbourne, taking with them as many servants as they would require while they were there.

They were to be there for several months, and while Agnes wheeled the perambulator up and down the front with an eye for every passing male, the family's rooms at the Manor were swathed in dust-sheets and holland covers, the chandeliers were tied up in muslin, and Mrs. Grim put the younger servants on board wages and sent them home.

The gardeners were kept busy repairing the damage that the caterers had done to the lawns, and the gamekeepers began to cast up the birds that would be ready for slaughter in the autumn, when her ladyship's relations came to shoot over the late Squire's coverts, and down at the Rectory Polly worked hard to get everything clean, and helped Martha to pack up the belongings of the old Rector so that his family could see to the disposal of it all when the time came.

Workmen began to paint and paper in empty rooms and only sufficient furniture was left for their own needs, but when Emily made a few tentative enquiries as to what Polly would like to do after September she said she did not know. After a few abortive attempts at drawing her out Emily decided that the trouble up at the Manor must have gone deeper than she had imagined, and so she took Martha's advice and "let her bide."

It was not the injustice of her dismissal, however, that hurt Polly most: she had enough years behind her to give her a good character when she applied for another post, and she knew that Mrs. Grim would speak up for her. But out of all the other servants up at the Great House nobody, not even James, had sent word that they were sorry, or that they understood how badly she had been used, and it was this neglect that rankled and wounded.

Not a soul came near her, and she missed them all unbearably. She missed Winnie's gay chatter, and young Albert's whistle, she missed Nurse Crampton's wisdom, and Mrs. Grim's warm interest. She felt an outcast, a misfit in the big Rectory, where she was snubbed by old Martha and treated with distant kindliness by Mrs. Harrison. As for Mr. Charles she scarcely noticed if he looked her way or not. The time was past when she had sat reading fairy tales to the children down in the woods and he had watched and listened with a smile.

She allowed that he was handsome, but she felt uneasily that under the surface he was like Major Goodyer, with the pride of his cousin, Lady Augusta, and the aloof generosity of the old Squire. She had no wish to enter that world any more: they had cast her out on the day before Miss Ellen's wedding, and she had no desire to return to it. It was a cold world at heart, without compassion or warmth. There was only one place where she longed to be, only one heart that she longed to possess, only one person who could give her all she would ever need, and it seemed that he no longer cared about her or wanted her, that he no longer knew if she were alive or dead. . . .

On Sundays now, when she slipped into church beside old Martha, she examined the pews in front, her eyes searching for James among the menservants in the Manor pews. But he was not there, and she could not see his broad shoulders towering over the others, or his crisply curling black hair behind Mrs. Grim and Mary, the still-room maid, who had stayed behind to help the housekeeper with the jam- and jelly-making of the autumn.

James appeared to have taken himself to church elsewhere: maybe he had found a girl who was kinder to him than she had been. . . . Polly was so worried about him and his continual avoidance of her that she did not at first notice how empty the rest of the church was, Sunday after Sunday. She did not see, either, until a week or so had passed, how the villagers avoided her and the Rectory folk, not returning the timid smiles she gave them, but staring through her with hard eyes.

And then one day, on her way back from the Post Office, she came face to face with Mary, and she looked her straight in the face as if she were a stranger and did not see the hand that she held out to her, and this, coupled with the coldness shown to her a few minutes before by Winnie's aunt at the Post Office, made Polly think that somebody might have been blackening her character after she had left Lady Augusta's employment. She felt she had to find out if it was so, and who it was, and what they could have said, and she ran after Mary and asked her what the matter was.

"I never thought *you* would treat me like this, Mary!" she cried.

Mary stared at her flushed face and tearful eyes without any expression at all, and then she said briefly, "I think you know very well why I don't want to speak to you, Polly," and would have gone on if Polly had not caught her arm.

"No!" she cried. "Fair is fair and right is right ... you've got to tell me, Mary, what it is that you have against me! What am I supposed to have done to set you against me? I insist on knowing!"

"*You* insist, indeed!" The anger in Mary's eyes hurt and stung. "What right have you to talk to me like that after what has happened? Are you brazen, Polly ... or just a fool?"

Polly's hand dropped and her face went white.

"I don't know what you mean!" she said.

Mary shook her head, her eyes reproachful and sad. "Oh, but I think you do!" she said gently. "When it's all over the village that you are at the Rectory because of Mr. Charles. ..."

"Because of—" Polly caught her breath. "Mary ... what do you mean? ... You must tell me. ..."

Mary hesitated and then she said: "I only know what other people know, Polly, that Mr. Charles asked you to ... to go and live at the Rectory ... and that he has even said that he will marry you ... in his own good time, no doubt! Oh, Polly, you silly, stupid little girl ... you thought you were flying high when you set your cap at Mr. Charles, and I dare say he encouraged you in it too ... I'm not saying the fault was all on your side. We've heard all about it now ... that tea you had with him in Broughton, and the meetings down in the woods. ..."

"Stop!" Polly's young voice was suddenly high-pitched and shrill with outrage. "How dare you say such things? How dare you even think them?"

"But, my dear, it's only what the whole village is saying and thinking," said Mary, and this time Polly let her go.

She walked back to the Rectory with her thoughts in such a turmoil that she scarcely knew where she was going. In the midst of her horror at what Mary had said, however, she knew in her heart that she had been speaking the truth. Suddenly she could see where before she had been blind: the whispers and nudges in church, the glances in her direction, the cool kindliness of Mrs. Harrison fighting with the distress in her face when she spoke to her, the look in Mr. Charles's eyes. . . . Above all, that look! . . .

She shivered and walked more quickly, anxious to get inside the kitchen before she encountered anybody else, her whole body hot with shame as she imagined the conversations in the servants' hall at the Manor, and the silent thoughts in the gamekeeper's cottage. . . . No wonder nobody came near her. No wonder that James avoided her too. . . .

She changed her dress and sat down in the kitchen to polish the silver. Martha was going through the lists of china with Mrs. Harrison in the housekeeper's room and Polly was thankful to be alone. But she was not to be left in peace for long, even in this sanctuary, because after a few minutes she heard a step outside the back door, and looking up quickly from the plate-basket she saw James standing there.

"Good evening, Polly my dear," he said, his voice softening as it always did when he spoke to her. "I've come to say good-bye."

16

THE village gossip and Lady Augusta's anger against the curate-in-charge and the little housemaid, Polly Kettle, had not been long in reaching James's ears, and although his first instinct was to seek out young Mr. Harroby and black both his eyes for him, he held himself in check, avoiding the places where he was likely to meet him.

When Charles took a walk down to the head game-keeper's cottage, however, to find out why the hope of the Windover cricket eleven did not turn up to practice batting any more, James happened to be at home, and looked the young gentleman from the Rectory up and down with a rudeness that brought the blood to Charles's cheek. All he said, though, in excuse for his absence, was that he had been lending a hand in the harvest fields in the evenings.

"The whole team has fallen off so these last few weeks," complained Charles. "They can't all be working in the harvest fields, can they, James?"

James did not smile. "Maybe they think as I do, Mr. Charles," he said quietly. "Cricket is for schoolboys, I reckon, not for grown men. And some of us are having no more dealing with such truck."

Charles could not believe that this young man was the hitherto respectful and polite James Burke, but when he tried to reason with him James gently shut the door in his face and leant against it on the other side, trembling as if there was an ague in his great frame.

"James!" His mother came out of the kitchen beyond the living-room into which the front door opened. "Whatever has come over you, to speak to Mr. Charles like that? And to shut the door in his face. . . ."

"If I had not done so," said James, very low, "I'd have killed him, Mother."

She did not pretend to know what he meant.

"I can't think it's true, all the same," she said gently. "I can't, whatever folk say ... and I *won't* believe it, what is more! Not of our little Polly ... she wouldn't do such a thing, James."

"She's under his roof, isn't she?" said James. "She's very young ... and I dare say she was flattered ... and I dare say he will marry her, you know. He'll do the right thing by her, because he's a parson. ... But if he shouldn't marry her, Mother, then ..."

"Then what?" she asked, her face worried and anxious. "Then what will you do, James?"

But that he could not answer, because he was able to look down into the dark depths of his own heart, and what he saw there made him dreadfully and bitterly afraid.

It was this fear that induced him to apply for a situation as coachman in a gentleman's household in Lincolnshire: there was a cottage offered and a salary of nearly two pounds a week, and when James wrote his application he enclosed with it a testimonial obtained from Lady Augusta in Eastbourne.

"I am very disappointed with young Burke," she complained to Josey as she wrote it out. "His father and his uncle have been with us for thirty years. He could have stepped up into being coachman at Windover directly Briggs gives up."

"Which probably won't be for another thirty years," said Josey lightly. "Perhaps James has ambitions."

"In my young days servants were content with what they had," said Lady Augusta peevishly. "All this comes of preaching equality."

But Josey insisted that she should give James a good reference all the same, and on the strength of it he was engaged and told to present himself to his new employer on the last Monday in August.

He found when the time came that he could not leave Windover without a final look at Polly, and so he made

his way down to the Rectory that Friday evening and
tossed his goodbye into her lap and saw her face go red
and then white.

"Goodbye, James?" she stammered incredulously.
"Why . . . whatever for?"

He told her about the place that waited for him in Lincolnshire, and as she listened she tried not to feel cast off
and abandoned, and she did her best to fight the leaden
weight of depression that had settled on her.

"But why go so far away?" she asked. "Wasn't there
any places near here, James?"

"I dessay there might be. I didn't look." His eyes rested
on her inscrutably. "I reckon I wanted to get as far away
from Windover as I could, Polly."

"But . . . why?" She picked up her duster and began to
rub away industriously at her polishing, setting her small
teeth in her lip to stop its trembling.

"Because, as I told you before," he said quietly,
"there's only one girl I'd ever want to share a cottage with
me, Polly, either down here in Windover or up there in
Lincolnshire, and I'm not a fool. . . . It didn't need others
to tell me that you'd set your feet in other ways than
mine. I think I knew it when I saw you get out of the
same railway carriage with him that day in the summer.
Yes, I did see you, though I said nothing about it then or
since. Don't think I'm blaming you, Polly, my dear, because I'm not. He's not worthy of you, and never could
be, but if that's the road you want your life to take, that's
the road it will have to take. The ways of the gentry aren't
my ways, and never will be: I don't understand 'em, and,
please God, I never will. I only wanted a wife who would
love me wherever I was, who would be accustomed to a
cottage and a working man, who'd be waiting for me
when I came in of nights and have love for me in her
heart, and I've loved you, Polly, from the first night when
I left you there at the kitchen door up at the Manor, so
little and so frightened and alone. . . . There's some
gentlemen that profess to be on the side of the downtrod-
den and the poor, and then don't hesitate to steal a poor
man's greatest treasure if the whim takes 'em that way,

and if I stay down here in Windover I might do something desperate, Polly, and that's why I've got to go." He turned to the door, his cap gripped tightly in his hands. "Goodbye, Polly ... and God go with you, my dearest dear!"

He was gone before she could call him back, and she heard his boots grating on the path and then the back gate slam shut behind him. For another moment she sat there staring at the silver spread out on the table, the hard things he had said beating on her heart and hurting as much as she had hurt him in the past. And then she put down her head among the crested spoons and wept aloud.

It was about ten minutes later when Charles came into the drawing-room that was all that was left in the way of a sitting-room now to Emily in the nearly empty Rectory.

"I went to see the Bishop this afternoon, Cousin Emily," he said briskly. "There is a vacancy for a parson in a Canadian diocese and he is putting my name forward with a warm recommendation."

"Canada?" Emily dropped her needlework in her lap.

"Yes, Canada," he said shortly. "A country where men and women are judged on their own merits, and where a man must prove himself or go under, and where his wife will be accepted for herself, and not cut because she was a housemaid, or laughed at because she drops an aitch."

Emily was silent. The evening dusk was shading her face, and when at last she spoke her voice was devoid of feeling.

"So you intend to marry Polly?" she said, and gentle as she was she could not hide her disapproval. "Have you told your mother?"

"There was no need. Cousin Augusta told her about it long ago. Mother wrote me a seven-page letter, blotted with tears. Mother has always cried more easily than any other woman I've known: she cried me into accepting Cousin John's charity, she cried me into going up to Oxford at his expense, and she cried me into doing as he wished and going into the Church. But she could not cry me into taking the family living here, and she will not cry me out of marrying Polly." He smiled tenderly. "My

Blessed Damozel! I'm going to take her to a home where 'we two will live at once, one life; and peace shall be with us.' There's certainly no peace here in Windover."

"Oh, *Charles!*" Emily was impatient with him for his romanticism. "It's no good saying that I think you are right because I don't. You will never be happy with a girl like Polly Kettle, and neither will she be happy with you. You can take her where you like, but Polly will still be herself and you will still be you."

He frowned, as impatient as she was.

"So you are on Cousin Augusta's side?" he said coldly.

"On this occasion yes, because I must be," she replied with firmness.

"Well, I suppose I might have expected it. Inherent snobbery is inbred in women of your class, Cousin Emily. Polly is a lovely, sweet girl, and I am in love with her and I shall marry her." He set his chin obstinately, and, seeing it, she made a helpless gesture and began to fold her work and put it away in her work-box.

"If you cannot see sense for yourself, then I'm afraid it is too late for me to teach you," she said quietly, stabbing her needle into the padded back of the box and putting the thimble and scissors into their appointed places. "I think I should remind you, though, of one or two things that appear to have escaped your notice. Polly comes from generations of people who have worked with their hands and been content with simple things, with simple needs and pleasures. There's no shame in that, and I'm not saying there is," she added quickly as he made a movement of protest. "And whatever you may think, Charles, it isn't inherent snobbery that makes me point this out to you, but a genuine concern for two young people who are perhaps mutually attracted to each other, without knowing how deep—or how shallow—that attraction is. When people have to work for their daily bread in the way Polly's people have—her father was a private soldier, I think, and her mother a general servant—it makes the essential needs of their existence the most important things in their lives. They've never had time to stop and think, to read, or to learn from books. They are dependent on others for nearly every decision they make."

"What you are saying is simply that Polly is uneducated. You are right, of course, but it is not her fault and I shall educate her in time. It will be my privilege and joy to do it."

"You may be able to teach her the rudiments of education, but can you teach her to laugh at the things you laugh at, to appreciate things that are more than meat and drink to you? Don't think I'm asking this for your sake only: it is for her sake too. I am very fond of Polly."

He moved his shoulders quickly. "She is not a moron. She has a quick intelligence and will soon learn."

"But she will still not have your background. Do you think her eyes will meet yours across a table in ready understanding of a shared joke as Josey's do? You have generations of culture behind you, and Polly is just a little country girl from a cottage, educated in the village school and the servants' hall at the Manor. It won't work, whatever you may say."

"But I say that it will." He came to her and kissed her lightly, and she turned her head away so that he should not see the tears in her eyes. "Don't worry, Cousin Emily. Better-matched marriages than mine and Polly's have come to grief. Would you have me behave as Archie Goodyer behaved, seeking a rich wife at whatever cost to his self-esteem? That's not my way, my dear!"

"No, of course not." She got up, sighing. "Well, if you are so set on it there is no more that I can do. Do you wish to get it settled at once? Or have you spoken to Polly already?"

"Not yet. Will you send her to me, please, as you go upstairs?"

"Very well." She left the room and a few minutes later Polly came in a hurry, wondering what it was that he wanted with her, but directly he told her to close the door and come to him in the window she knew, and she gave a little gasp and stayed where she was with her back to the door, her hands spread out against its panels for protection and support.

Seeing that she was too frightened to come to him, he went to her instead, and was amused and a little annoyed because she turned her head away, like a trapped creature searching for escape.

"Don't look so scared, Polly, my love!" he said, smiling. "I'm not going to eat you! I have been telling Mrs. Harrison that I'm in love with you, and that I mean to marry you. I hope she did not frighten you when she sent you to me here? I know she does not approve of it, but the approval of others has never mattered to me and never will, thank God." He paused but she did not reply, and as she seemed to be struggling for words, he went on more tenderly, "*Did* she frighten you, little Polly?"

"No, she never said nothing." She hung her head, her face crimsoning, and thinking that she was too overcome to give him the answer he wanted, he took her hands in his.

"Well, then," he said. "Have you nothing to say to me?"

The touch of his hands seemed to spur her into action. She snatched them away and burst out at him:

"So they were right about you . . . if they weren't right about me! No wonder they talked and stared at me . . . no wonder they wouldn't speak to me, and didn't come to church any more! Oh, Mr. Charles, how could you take advantage of me like that and make me a laughing-stock for the village? I didn't think it of you . . . I didn't really. . . ."

"Take advantage of you? Make you a laughing-stock?" His indignation was touched with anger as he put his hands on her shoulders and gave her a little shake. "What on earth are you talking about, Polly, and what is the matter with you? I want to marry you, child! Can't you get that into your head?"

It was obvious that he expected her to view the prospect with delight, gratitude, and humility, but there was no longer any gratitude, and not much humility left in Polly. She was filled with self-reproach and hurt pride, and as she remembered Mary's words, and the way James had looked at her when he came to say goodbye, her anguished heart felt that it must burst. She turned on

Charles furiously, hatred in the brimming eyes that stared up into his handsome face.

"But I don't want to marry you!" she cried. "And what is more nothing would make me marry you, Mr. Charles! You have done your best to take away my character, and I suppose as you're a clergyman you feel you've got to marry me because of it, but you're no better really than that Major Goodyer—" She broke off. "Oh; let me go, and leave me alone!"

She twisted herself out of his hands, got the door open and herself outside it, and ran through the hall to the kitchen. The side door into the yard was open, and beyond it the yard gate separated the Rectory from the world that had been her own world, and full of friendly, kindly faces, until the Harrobys made it hard and unkind.

Catching her breath in a sob she got the gate open and was through it, and ran off down the lane, leaving it to crash behind her. On she sped, down the path that led across the meadows by the church, and beyond the church to the edge of the woods where they skirted the park, and through the woods to the clearing where the head game-keeper had his cottage, where a large young man was sitting on a bench chopping firewood for his mother and smoking an old briar pipe.

She stopped short then, and he looked up and put down his pipe on the bench beside him, his grey eyes suddenly alert.

"Hullo," said James. "Where are you running to in such a hurry then, my dear?"

"James!" She came the few yards that still separated them more slowly, until she was so near that she could have touched him, and then she stood still, looking down wistfully into his brown face and remembering all the times she had seen it, from the first icy evening when he had put a rug round her shoulders, and the winter's morning when he had comforted a weeping child with a bruised face in the potting-shed, to the evening last June when he had asked her to marry him and she had laughed at him for it.

She said humbly: "You said some things to me this

evening and they weren't true. There's no call for anybody in this village to think that Mr. Charles would have to marry me, because it isn't so. .... I thought he was only being sorry for me, and kind, when Mrs. Harrison asked me to go there to help old Martha pack up the Rectory things. .... I never dreamed that anybody would think ... what they have thought about me and Mr. Charles—" She broke off. "Oh, James, *don't* just sit there making me feel so awkward and so wicked. .... Say something to me! Please, please do!"

But he did not say anything at all. He put down the chopper beside his pipe, and he got up and took her into his arms and held her close, and she clung to him, feeling the strength of his protection and his love, and she knew that for the rest of her life she was safe and secure, and defended against every peril that the world had to offer.

Emily Harrison was changing her dress for dinner when she heard the distant slam of the yard gate, and looking out from behind the lace curtains she saw Polly's flying figure, without cap or apron, tearing off across the meadows. She watched her until she was out of sight and then she went on with her dressing, wondering why she had gone off in a hurry like that, and not even thinking that she might have refused Charles. Like her young cousin, it had never occurred to her that such a thing would be possible, and she was far more inclined to believe, with a sinking heart, that Polly, beside herself with delight and importance, had run off to tell all her friends in the village and to boast of her conquest of young Mr. Charles.

The news would not only give the village something to talk about, she thought bitterly: there wouldn't be one of their friends in the whole county who wouldn't fasten on to it with the same delight.

She waited until dinner was served before putting in an appearance in the dining-room, and was surprised to find Charles there with a face like a thundercloud. He did not speak to her, however, and Martha waited on them alone, and Emily fancied that the young man's glum silence meant that she was not forgiven for her well-meant meddling in his affairs.

When the meal was finished he mumbled an excuse about having letters to write and went away and shut himself into the study. Emily, completely mystified by his behavior, asked Martha to send Polly to her directly she came in.

"Do you happen to know where she went to, Martha?" she asked, and wondered if Martha knew more than she thought when she replied sourly that she had probably slipped out to meet a sweetheart.

"Them girls that is used to service in the big houses like the Manor is all the same when they get with one or two servants in a gentleman's house," she said. "There's no holding them. . . . They puts on such airs, and they think they're answerable to nobody. It wouldn't occur to Polly that she ought to ask *me* before she ran out like that."

When Polly returned, however, at a little after ten o'clock there was no sign of repentance about her as she knocked at Emily's door. Mrs. Harrison told her to come in and waited until she had shut the door behind her before she spoke with grave displeasure.

"Martha and I were worried about you, Polly," she said. "We could not think where you had gone."

"I'm sorry, madam." Polly lifted her head and her eyes were starry with happiness. "There was somebody I had to see . . . to ask him what I should do, I mean. And he says I ought to give in my notice at once, ma'am, because I'm going to be married."

Emily's spirits drooped. She had been right then, and Charles's gloom at dinner had been directed against herself, while, as for this girl, there would not be a soul in the village who would not know by this time of her engagement to young Mr. Harroby. "You . . . are going to be married?" she repeated tonelessly.

"Yes, ma'am. And as he's got a long journey in front of him on Monday, there was many things we had to talk about."

"Monday?" Emily was surprised. Charles must have got his plans more advanced than she had imagined.

"Yes, ma'am. I'm ever so sorry that it's such short no-tice, but James thinks I ought to go home to my Auntie Ada for a week or two until he's made our home ready for us, and it will give me time to be asked in church and all. I'd like to be asked in Moccrington, because that was where I lived before I came to the Manor."

"James?" What in the world was the girl talking about?

"Yes, ma'am . . . James Burke. He's got a post as coachman to a gentleman in Lincolnshire, and he's going off there on Monday. So I thought, ma'am, if you don't mind, and seeing as you are so near moving out of here, and that most of the cleaning is done, I'd give in my no-tice and go to my Auntie Ada on Monday too. . . ."

James Burke . . . young James, so large and silent, with his big hands like silk on the reins. . . .

"But *of course* you may go, Polly!" In her relief and ecstasy Emily could have hugged the girl. "I did not quite understand what was happening, and who you were to marry. But now that I know, of course it will be all right for you to leave whenever you like, and I hope you will be very happy with James."

"Thank you, ma'am." Polly's face was radiant in the light of Emily's candles. "I know I shall, because I've al-ways loved him, ma'am, and he's always loved me, ever since that horrid old cook they had at the Manor hit me and bruised my face."

Somebody else had bruised that pretty face just lately, but they did not speak about that.

"We shall be very sorry to lose you, Polly," said Emily gently.

Polly shook her head.

"Martha will be pleased," she said. "She will be glad to have you to herself again. And you will be glad to get home again, ma'am, I know."

"And Mr. Charles?" said Emily, unable to resist the implication, but Polly only laughed.

"Mr. Charles, ma'am, if you will excuse me saying so, is just a little bit spoilt. At least, that's what James says. He thinks he reads too much of those books of his, and

James, he don't hold with too much book-learning. He says it's the way we live what counts. And as James was coming home with me just now we saw Mr. Charles sitting there in the study, working at his sermon I expect, and I remembered that old pile of the late Rector's sermons what we were turning out of that cupboard in the study the other day, Martha and me, and I said to James what a pity it was that Mr. Charles didn't read them in church of a Sunday instead of making up his own. Nobody would ever know they'd heard 'em before, and it's what the village is more used to, you know, ma'am. The old Rector did preach such beautiful sermons, and I'm sure if he was alive today he'd say Mr. Charles was kindly welcome."

"I'll suggest it to him, Polly," said Emily, her mouth twitching a little. She added, because she was full of curiosity about it all, "You know, I thought Mr. Charles wanted to marry you, Polly!"

"He may have thought he did, ma'am," said Polly with a slight blush. "In a way he reminds me of Miss Susan, who would always go for the outside of the cake."

"You mean that the prettier the icing, the more she thought she wanted it?" said Emily shrewdly.

"Well, in a way, ma'am." Polly looked confused. "I think some gentlemen only see the sugar icing, meaning no offense to Mr. Charles, I'm sure. He'll do a lot better when he's learned a bit of wisdom."

"You might have taught him more than he could teach you, Polly," said Emily, discovering this for the first time. "You've got a wise little head on your shoulders."

"But I'm not a lady, ma'am!" cried Polly, her eyes round with reproach, but at the same moment she laughed with all the gaiety and wickedness of the eternal Eve.

"Polly," said Emily, half laughing herself and half exasperated too, "You're a baggage! Go upstairs to bed. ... No, wait a moment before you go!" She found her purse and took from it five golden sovereigns and put them into the girl's hand. "For a wedding present," she said, and reaching up she kissed her cheek.

Emily left for home at the end of September, taking Martha with her, and it was still a very angry young man who set out for the late afternoon train for London on the same day.

The truth was that as the days passed Polly's refusal had turned Charles's anger against himself: the spell was broken, and he saw his Blessed Damozel for what she was, a very pretty little housemaid who had sent his senses swimming during the magical days of the summer.

Lady Augusta's pen had been busy during her stay in Eastbourne, and it seemed that his behavior had not only earned her contempt, but that of the neighborhood. Pretty girls no longer flocked to Windover church, and the Windovers themselves had left Broughton Park for Scotland, taking Anna with them.

But the opinions of Lady Augusta and her friends were nothing to Charles: it was Josey's silence that condemned him most, although he knew that he deserved it.

It was with grief, apprehension, and joy therefore that he saw her bicycle approaching the station on that last afternoon, a few minutes before his train was due. Except for himself and his piled-up luggage the platform was empty: the stationmaster and the only porter were busy in the Parcels Office, and did not even see Miss Harroby arrive.

"Charles!" She left her bicycle leaning against the palings and ran down the platform to him breathlessly. "I had a letter from Aunt Emily telling me that you were off today, and I made the excuse that I had to come home to see Graves about some plants she wanted for her garden. But really I had to see you . . . to say goodbye."

"Oh, Josey, my dear!" It went to her heart to see how humble he was—her arrogant, light-hearted Charles. "You know about . . ." Words failed him miserably.

"About Polly? Yes, Charles, I know."

He could not justify himself to her, but he had to try. "Some madness got into me . . . I couldn't help it. . . ."

She smiled disarmingly. "But most of the Harrobys are romantics at heart. Look how Ellen grieved over that impossible young man, Roger Blackstone."

Why was it that she knew instinctively the words that would comfort him?

"And you?" he said. "Are you a romantic, Josey?"

"Oh," she said lightly, "I am the practical one of the family. Did you never guess?"

"Well, I did in a way. And I thanked God for it. The family needs a bit of common sense." The signal arm dropped with a clatter and he looked down at her with despair. Now that the moment of parting had come there were so many things he had to say to her and so little time in which to say them.

"I'll write to you," she promised him, trying to interpret what was in his mind. "When you let me have your address in Canada. . . ."

"Writing isn't enough." The smoke of the train was in sight now, over the cutting. He blurted out, "Josey . . . if I make a go of things out there . . . will you come out to me?"

She stood very still.

"But, Charles, you'll find yourself a wife . . . some pretty Canadian girl. . . ."

"It's you I want." Whatever Polly Kettle may or may not have taught him, somehow he had learned humility as well. "I know I'm not good enough for you, Josey . . . but these last weeks when I thought I'd lost you have been hell. I want to have you with me always, to give me strength, to put me right, to keep me from getting swollen-headed." He turned away. "I know it's hopeless, though, and you could never care for me in that way."

Her eyes rested on his broad shoulders tenderly as she thought how vulnerable he was, and that it was as a governess that he needed her, not as a wife.

"My dear," she said gently, "a wife has to be something more than a prop and an antidote for a man's vanity! But if it will comfort you, I promise that I'll think about it, and if you still feel the same in a year's time . . . you can ask me again. . . ." If she had not loved him so much she could never have left the door open for him: she would have snatched happiness while she could, but he did not see it that way. She had given him hope and he had to catch at it before it was too late.

The train was on the metals just beyond the platform, slowing down, the smoke thin against the blue autumn sky, and he caught her hand in his.

"In a year's time I'll never love you more than I love you now ... don't you understand? I *love* you, Josey, and I didn't know it until these last terrible weeks when I thought I'd never see you again. If I have to face life without you I ... I'll come out of the Church altogether ... I'll go to the bad : ... I don't know what I'll do. ..."

"Love?" she said. "But that's different. ..." Her face was radiant, her eyes were suddenly alight, and seeing it he took a deep breath.

"You mean ... you will?"

She nodded, and his head went up and he laughed aloud, and then scowled as the train came to a standstill. "Confound this damned train! There's so much to do ... so much to say. ..." The porter came hurrying down towards them and he turned to him quickly, giving his orders. "Ted, get Miss Josey's bicycle and put it in the van with my luggage. And label it for London, and get another first-class ticket for London, and hurry. There's not a lot of time."

Ted ran off and was soon back with the bicycle and brought the extra ticket to where Charles was helping his cousin into an empty first-class carriage.

"Thank you, Ted," Charles dived into his pocket. "And get that luggage loaded ... and the best of luck to you."

"And the same to you, sir." Ted hurried away and Josey said:

"Charles, what are you doing? ... And where do you think you are taking me?"

"To my mother. She'll cry all over you, so you are in for a damp time, but it won't be for long. Only as long as it will take us to get a special license and Raymond up from his slum to marry us."

"But, Charles ... I haven't any clothes. ... ."

"Grimmie will send them on, and you can borrow from the girls until they arrive."

Josey sank down on the cushioned seat and laughed.

"You've thought of everything, haven't you?" she said.

"No. But it will come to me as we travel on." He gave her an answering grin as he climbed in beside her. "I'm just not risking losing you again."

The engine pulled out of the station and Ted said to the stationmaster, "If I didn't think it was impossible, I'd say Mr. Charles was eloping with Miss Josey."

The stationmaster stroked his side-whiskers thoughtfully.

"And I'd say more impossible things than that have happened," he said. "And, what is more, it's a pity he didn't do it years ago."

The red-cheeked apples on the trees that overhung the country station, the golden chestnuts beyond them, and the ragged sunflowers in front, all seemed to say that the summer was dying fast, and that it was just as well to bury it and be done with now.

But the two travelling on in the train for London had no thought for the summer that had gone. Charles's arm was round Josey's waist and her head was on his shoulder, and for them life was just beginning in the countless summers that lay ahead.

ALSO BY MARY ANN GIBBS

THE ROMANTIC FRENCHMAN

Miss Cheriton hoped that one of the young French officers on parole in Doverton would help to raise her dear niece's spirits after an unhappy love affair. But unfortunately Lieutenant Philippe Cadot was not interested in Melissa Prestwick. All his attention was held by the fascinating Lady Tamporley, still beautiful but married so young that she already had five children. And in the brief English spring a bittersweet romance blossomed between them.

Meanwhile fate was taking a hand in Melissa's affairs. The man she had jilted reappeared, courting another girl. And although Mel was still smarting from being taken for granted, her heart started to soften towards her former beau.

HORATIA

Horatia Pendleton stood to inherit a fortune when she came of age – if she lived that long. Her wicked uncle was plotting to marry her off to a friend or dispose of her in a more permanent fashion.

Reluctantly Horatia turned her back on Newcross, the only home she had ever known. In just four months' time she would be twenty-one and mistress of her fortune. In the meantime she must disguise herself and hope that her uncle wouldn't find her.

But Horatia, outspoken and independent, was never good at keeping quiet. Dashing Mr. Latimer found that she irritated him exceedingly when he came to pay court to the sweet young daughter of the house. For there was Horatia, a runaway heiress, flouting the conventions by masquerading as a stableboy.

THE PENNILESS HEIRESS

Mary Ann Gibbs

When the Brighton coach pulled into the Two Apprentices yard, Harriet Strangeways arrived in London. She was a red-haired little girl, travelling alone – and no-one came to collect her. In her broad country accent she told Martin that her uncle, Sir Everard Maltby, was supposed to be meeting her. And Martin, who hid a soft heart beneath his brash young man-about-town exterior took pity on the child.

Martin had no way of knowing that, by offering Harriet shelter for the night, he was establishing himself as her guardian. Sir Everard refused to accept that she was the heiress to Maltby Cross and Harriet was put in the charge of Martin's formidable aunt, the Dowager Lady Eddicombe.

As the years passed, Harriet grew into a breathtaking beauty, whose rumoured fortune made her the talk of the town. But to Martin she was still just little Harriet Strangeways ...

CORONET BOOKS

THE APOTHECARY'S DAUGHTER

Mary Ann Gibbs

A vast social gulf divided Hugo Vigilant, Lord Vigilant's cousin and heir to the great house of Marischall, from Susanna Hayter, the local apothecary's daughter. Hugo saw only a rebellious child who had just been expelled from school. Dismissing Susanna, his thoughts returned to pretty but spoilt Camilla, the eminently suitable heiress who was to become his wife.

But Hugo had reckoned without Lord Vigilant. And when he discovered that the old rake was taking a particular interest in Susanna, he was forced to voice his disapproval. But the self-willed old rogue took no notice of Hugo, nor of the local gossip his attentions were causing. As far as Lord Vigilant was concerned, all that mattered was that he was becoming very fond of pretty Susanna Hayter . . .

CORONET BOOKS

ALSO AVAILABLE IN CORONET BOOKS

MARY ANN GIBBS

☐ 18985 1	The Romantic Frenchman	35p
☐ 18984 3	Horatia	35p
☐ 19349 2	The Penniless Heiress	35p
☐ 19943 1	The Apothecary's Daughter	45p

NORAH LOFTS

☐ 15111 0	The King's Pleasure	35p
☐ 16950 8	A Rose For Virtue	35p
☐ 16216 3	Lovers All Untrue	30p
☐ 19352 2	Crown Of Aloes	40p
☐ 17826 4	Charlotte	40p
☐ 18403 5	Nethergate	40p

JOSEPHINE EDGAR

☐ 18784 0	My Sister Sophie	35p
☐ 18783 2	The Dark Tower	35p
☐ 18782 4	Time Of Dreaming	35p

*All these books are available at your local bookshop or newsagent,
or can be ordered direct from the publisher. Just tick the titles you
want and fill in the form below.*

CORONET BOOKS, P.O. Box 11, Falmouth, Cornwall.
Please send cheque or postal order, and allow the following for
postage and packing:
UK AND EIRE—15p for the first book plus 5p per copy for each
additional book ordered to a maximum charge of 50p.
OVERSEAS CUSTOMERS AND B.F.P.O.—please allow 20p for the
first book and 10p per copy for each additional book.

Name ....

Address ....

....